I0642386

Frank Arthur Putnam

Living in the World, With Other Ballads and Lyrics

Frank Arthur Putnam

Living in the World, With Other Ballads and Lyrics

ISBN/EAN: 9783744782708

Printed in Europe, USA, Canada, Australia, Japan

Cover: Foto ©Andreas Hilbeck / pixelio.de

More available books at **www.hansebooks.com**

Living in the World

with

Other Ballads and Lyrics

By

Frank Putnam

Chicago and New York

Rand, McNally & Company

mdcccxcix

DEDICATION.

To whosoever has drunk the wine
  Of light-heart Love in a care-free fashion;
To whosoever has felt the fine,
  Pure, fair delight of a blameless passion;

To whosoever has dreamed him dreams;
  To him whom Hope has said good morrow;
To him whose blood for his country streams;
  To her who sits in the dark with Sorrow.

To good and bad and the half-way folk,
  Who would if they dared but fear transgression,—
Come robed in light, or in mask and cloak:
  Here none is harried to make confession.

To any my friends who have wished me gain;
  To my enemies all, revealed or hidden,—
Here's welcome frank in a homely strain:
  Saint and sinner alike are bidden.

To man and maid, to mother and child,
  Torn from the clay to wear Time's tether:—
Here life looks higher, by faith beguiled,
  Where all sorts sit at the board together.

PREFACE.

(Ballad of the Poet's Desire to be Rich.)

O, a pitiful experience it is
    To wear the chains and hear the Muses calling;
The agony reflected on the phiz
    Of the victim is amazing and appalling.

He would like to cut a figure in the world,
    And he'd like to tread the highlands of Parnassus;
But—the Devil was behind the gun that hurled
    The poet through the secret misty passes.

He will tell you, if you listen, he despises
    The sordid gauds that fill his neighbors' eyes,
That his high mission is not to the prizes,
    But, just between the two of us, he lies.

For he has a thousand hungers in his heart
    That saner men would laugh at if they knew:
A cabin in a forest far apart
    From the city's grim, iconoclastic crew;

A sweetheart—and a new one now and then—
    To sympathize with all his noble notions,
To idolize the creatures of his pen,
    And mix for him his Heliconic potions.

PREFACE.

The poet is a sultan—in his mind;
   He swims the starry vastness—in his trances;
Alas, that one of his ethereal kind
   Must beg the man who prints him for advances.

The thousand hungry hungers I have hinted
   Are not the only miseries he knows;
No sooner does he get a vision printed
   Than he meets some heartless person whom he owes.

The poet has a family, of course,
   For Poverty was never less than fertile;
Nine sturdy little shavers on the force,
   He hopes will hew the oak and shun the myrtle.

He prays that they inherit from the mater
   The solid sense that gives a man control;
That they, in rubbing up against a frater,
   Will touch his pocket rather than his soul.

In short, and in conclusion, at the center,
   He is not so fantastic as he seems;
The Muse of Song—he says it—is his mentor,
   But yellow tints the purple of his dreams.

CONTENTS.

INTRODUCTION.

It is a bold man or, at least, a man trustful of the public, who in this era of feverish practicality dares have printed a volume of his poems. But real poetry is not dead, and will never die. It will but grow in its Homeric rank. While the world grows in thought and keen perception and sensibility there will come with every year throughout the coming ages more and more of those who will understand what poetry is and who will delight and revel in it and be helped by it.

Poetry is not mere rhyme. There are many rhymers, but few poets. Frank Putnam is a poet. He has a claim upon the world and the world has a claim upon him.

STANLEY WATERLOO.

Chicago, August 18, 1899.

LIVING IN THE WORLD

LIVING IN THE WORLD.

Nothing equal to it as a training for the heart,—
Sympathy is waning in the man who dwells apart;

Learning he may gather from the pages of the wise—
(Learning with a mighty big percentage of it lies!)

I prefer the open way where men and women meet,
Grumbling in the gloomy days and smiling in the
      sweet;

Hindering or helping, each according to his light,
(Maybe I'm mistaken and the other man is right.)

Sympathize with each of them, the gentle and the
      stern;
Time enough for all of us to live and lose and learn.

Even in the meanest I can see the hand divine;
Qualities that make them mean are duplicates of mine.

The narrow-breasted angel with a virtue that is grim,
He didn't pick his spirit, so I sympathize with him.

2

True, he knows the party at the gate will let *him*
    through,
But think how *much* he worries on account of me and
    you.

He who has the gentle heart will oftenest be hurt;
Easier to wound him than a man of common dirt.

Has a higher happiness when happiness he wins;
Has a deeper misery when misery begins.

Woman with the heavy heart and sorrow in your eyes,
Humankind are merciless but love is in the skies.

Stumbled, little sister, when you didn't know the road;
Spring of joy welled up in you so fast it overflowed.

I, shall I condemn you with a stony-fronted frown?
No, my dear, I love you for the love that led you
    down.

Sister are you sorrowful?   Brother are you sad?—
Stumbled and the heart of you may never more be
    glad?

Cheery up my dearies and in years that are to be
Days of fair serenity may dawn for you and me.

Sinners in the choir loft and sinners in the pew,—
Parson's interceding and the Lord'll see us through.

Sexton has a cottage in a cozy little lot;
Tenants of the sexton are speedily forgot.

Though we walk in weariness until the very end,
Though we quit the weary world with none to call us
    friend,

Dear old Mother Nature, with a mother's soothing
    charms,
Lulls her tired children into slumber in her arms.

She has love for all of us, the wise ones and the wild,
Greeting us at evening with "Welcome home, my
    child!"

Wicked hearts and sorry hearts, and happy hearts im-
    pearled—
Nothing teaches charity like living in the world.

SONG IN PRAISE OF POVERTY.

A song in praise of poverty:
   Not grinding want that fills with hate
   The belly robbed to glut the great,
   Nor slavish toil in mean estate,
But independent poverty.

A song in praise of poverty:
   A rusty coat, say you? It hides
   A heart as gay as groom's or bride's;
   No envious hate therein abides:
A royal robe is poverty.

A song in praise of poverty:
   No lands or houses call I mine,
   At my board water flows for wine,
   Yet I have many a friendship fine:
A royal grace has poverty.

A song in praise of poverty:
   The lass who lies within my arms
   Surrendered all her peerless charms
   For love and not for bonds or farms:
A royal proof is poverty.

A song in praise of poverty :
   The simple joys that I must sieze
   Would have no power to pique or please
   Had I been born to idle ease :
A royal spur is poverty.

A song in praise of poverty :
   The Lord my God was good to me ;
   Alloting what He would to me,
   He gave the best He could to me—
The royal gift of poverty !

CONTENT.

Content with toil that's half a song,
   To no ambitions bound,
In jovial mood I tramp along
   Toward the common ground.

THE SONGS OF ROBERT BURNS.

We view afar the mighty souls above Andean snows,
Whose splendid lines to humbler minds the charms of
    art disclose;
These dignify prosperity, but when the current turns,
We find a brother's welcome in the heart of Robert
    Burns.

Art's glorious aristocracy let serve the bookish clan
Who rate a polished metaphor above the rights of
    man;
I love him best who sang the worth of Poverty's con-
    cerns—
The peer of nature's poets and her princes, Robert
    Burns.

I love him for his human faults, God knows they cost
    him dear;
For every hour of folly Fate decreed a bitter tear.
And man shall prize his memory all time, since each
    discerns
His own heart's vibrant passions in the songs of Rob-
    ert Burns.

Though Pecksniffs turn in pious wrath from fiery
    strains that thrill,

And frigid critics warn him off the Muses' sacred hill,

The hand of truth-preserving Time these paltry creat-
    ures spurns,

And lays a wreath of laurel on the brow of Robert
    Burns.

TO JEAN NICOT, THE SMOKER'S SAINT.

"It is somewhat odd that none of the long list of smoking poets has sung the praises of Jean Nicot, the French diplomat, for whom was named Nicotiana, the weed of great delight."—*Chicago Times-Herald.*

Illustrious Sir, whom the All-Seer
    Located back in earlier ages,
To you I bow in reverence here,
    Thou first among my favorite sages.

Earth's rule, I know, is to forget
    (If truth hath come from her detractors)
The useful sons of men; and yet,
    You rank among her benefactors.

And can it be that vandal Time,
    Whose ruthless hands ne'er know inaction,
Shall ever lessen the sublime
    Delights of your dear benefaction?

Ah, no, sweet Sir! then rest at peace
    In whatsoever tomb they laid you.
With splendid fame (since your release)
    A grateful world hath well repaid you.

Wherever comrades share their wine;
  Where sits the scholar, meditating;
Where sailors rove the rolling brine;
  Where students drink their beer, debating;

Where lightly treads the wily scout,
  Alert against whatever ill be;
Where soldiers pace the grim redoubt—
  Your name is loved and ever will be.

Oft at the time eve's gray enshrouds
  In somber garb the quiet hours,
Have I, up through the fleecy clouds,
  Seen Florist Fancy's fairest flowers.

Your health, good sir, I gladly pledge
  In this long, fragrant, moist Havana,
And my true faith to you allege,
  Whose name adorns nicotiana.

*   *   *   *   *

What mockery's in that "long, moist" weed!
  You understand, Jean, I was joking;
A corncob pipe's about my speed
  Whenever I'm inclined to smoking.

But even so, shall none give praise
  Where due? If yes, what purse-proud puffer
Could do the trick? Ah! duty lays
  That task on some poor rhyming duffer.

So runs the world. The few may eat
  Of pleasure's substance, but the many
Must think joy's shadow's shadow sweet
  And buy it with their pauper's penny.

The rhymer's task is to deceive
  By painting want in pleasing colors;
To filch the grief from them that grieve
  And rob dull life of half its dolors;

To make the husk seem golden grain;
  Inspire the roofless wretch with sorrow
That others out in misery's rain
  Share not his hope of happy morrow.

*   *   *   *   *   *   *

Long years have flown since you lay down,
  Quitting nicotiana sadly,
But never singer wove thee crown,
  Where many should have wrought it gladly.

Let then this tribute, rude but warm,
  Unworthy of its inspiration,
Claiming no grace of thought or form,
  Receive thy *friendly* commendation.

And let me add, ere farewell's said,
  The ills you had you bravely bore 'em;
So I'll fling naught at Fortune's head,
  But smoke my pipes and thank God for 'em.

JOHN AND DARIUS GREEN.

Darius Green and his flying machine
   Were given to fame in the years gone by;
Now comes before us one Jonathan Green—
A Green whose equal has never been seen—
   Not even Darius, for John *can* fly.

Darius believed he could cleave the air
   With wings of leather and wire—and luck;
The day was sunny, and calm, and fair
When Darius sailed, but alas! nowhere
   Was the earth so hard as the spot he struck.

Darius, in failure, achieved his desire,
   And proved to the world he was right in his mind,
By mounting the skies, ever higher and higher;
But he left his harness of leather and wire—
   Left that and his battered-up clay behind.

John Green knew better—no heaven for him;
   The earth was as high as he cared to go.
He chose a day when the sky was dim,
When winds howled over him, wild and grim,
   And *he* did fly, and by no means slow.

Whew! how his wheels did whistle around!
  One-twenty-five was his time for a mile.
A long grey line and a murmuring sound
Of his bicycle streaking it over the ground.
  Nothing the matter with John Green's style!

THE CORNCOB CENTER SAGE.

There's a misty sort of pleasure
   In a quiet backward glance
To the half-forgotten sorrows
   Of the seasons that are sped,
But the world is moving forward
   And your solitary chance
To acquire the things you're after
   Is in looking straight ahead.

Half of life is light and gladness
   And the other half is pain ;
God's eternal sense of fairness
   To his creatures here below
Makes this ruling universal,
   So there's nothing you can gain
By bewailing your misfortunes
   Or by cherishing your woe.

Don't give up to somber dreaming ;
   While the years are flying fast,
Better far by stern ambition
   To be tyrannously led

Than to sit a-holding inquests
   On the failures of the past.
Keep a-planning then, and digging
   And a-looking straight ahead.

If your mind's so constituted
   That you're always seeing grief,
And the ready tears of sympathy
   You're happy to be giving
Don't you waste 'em on the people
   Who are dead and past relief,
But expend 'em in the service
   Of the luckless now a-living.

Half the melancholy persons
   Who are sighing by the way
Would be finding life a pleasure
   And a benefit instead,
If they'd give their whole attention
   To the work in hand today—
Just a-digging and a-planning
   And a-looking straight ahead.

THE BANQUET.

On this night in the dusk of my innermost chamber
A reception is holden—come in, you were bidden.
In the contact of spirit and flesh I salute you.
You are welcome, you brother, you sister, none alien.
Whether virgin or scarlet no matter, I love you.

You that haughtily halt at the doorway awaiting
Special sign, do you dream I will meet you with fawn-
      ing?
Do you fancy the glitter of wealth or of station,
Or the fame universal whose halo proclaims you,
Will impel me to set you apart from these others?

For an answer I raise up this wretch from the gutter;
Him I heartily clasp with the grip of affection.

Yea, depart if it please you, contemptuous, I care not,
To the scenes of ephemeral triumphs returning;
We shall surely make merry this evening without you.
Does it seem to you, friends, that my chamber is nar-
      row
For the multitude thronging the hallway, approach-
      ing?
Never fear; we shall find it commodious, sufficient;
To the right, to the left, there is room for all comers.

You that slave in the sun that another may pluck
    you—
You that sigh in the Shadows of Silence, cease, enter—
To the banquet of Love in my heart I invite you.

NATIONAL FOLLIES.

Small wonder old-world peoples laugh
  At our immense pretensions ;
They see that we, though meaning well,
  Default from our intentions.

While corporations loot the land,
  All silent sit our writers ;
But press and legislature leap
  To stop a pair of fighters.

We give away the public streets
  And pay a toll to use 'em,
Then only talk when men who hold
  These privileges abuse 'em.

"Political equality,"
  We oft declare is vital ;
How charmingly we prove it so
  By worshipping a title.

"Republican simplicity"
  Continually we're boasting ;
But titled foreign visitors
  Grow weary of our toasting.

Our "ballot pure" and "freemen's rights"
   We flaunt in foreign faces;
Yet brazen thieves we tolerate
   In honorable places.

No man who steals our water by
   The tun becomes a felon,
But woe betide the dusky wretch
   Who steals a watermelon!

Could savage Patagonians
   Politically view us,
I half suspect they'd quickly send
   Their missionaries to us.

A CLASSIC.

'Tis a record of olden-time dreamings or deeds
That each one of us owns and that nobody reads.

THE POET'S DILEMMA.

Genius fleers at the common rules,
And so makes sure of the scorn of fools.

Talent conforms, accepts the laws,
And wins the hurrying mob's applause.

Mobs and their fads are soon forgot;
The rebel who scoffed and starved is not;

On his lean body a stone men raise;
They sing his songs and they chant his praise.

Still stupid as ever are men today;
They treat live gods in the same old way.

The lesson in this, it appears to me,
Is: Grub or Glory, which shall it be?

Do you want to be known and bought and read
What time you're living, or mourned for dead?

You can't have both and you may get neither;
Lucky enough is the man with either.

So make your choice while the hour remains :—
Which shall it be, now, belly or brains?

BALLAD OF EMANCIPATED SOULS.

INTRODUCTORY.

We're Hungry Ike
　　And Weary Bill;
We never worked—
　　We never will.

The hedge our roof,
　　The sod's our cot,
An oyster can's
　　Our coffee pot.

We break our fast
　　At break o' day,
Then hoist our traps
　　And go our way.

We revel in
　　Fair nature's moods;
We're long on joys
　　If short on foods.

Our life is free—
  We skip the towns;
No copper fierce
  Upon us frowns.

We make no bluff
  About hard times;
The '73
  Or other crimes.

We do not claim
  That we refrain
From work to save
  Our fellows pain;

That jobs may fall
  In other hands,
We but obey
  The Lord's commands.

Man was not born
  To toil and sweat;
We bow to fate
  With no regret.
We're Hungry Ike
  And Weary Bill;
We never worked—
  We never will.

PHILOSOPHIC.

Good morning, Judge,
  You see we're back
Along the old
  Familiar track.
The same old Ike,
  The same old Bill,
Who hold their old
  Convictions still.

You understand
  We don't assert
That honest toil
  Is apt to hurt
The average man's
  Mere fleshly bowl
But, ah! it soils
  His precious soul.

Eh! what's that, judge—
  You ain't been sick?
Well, me and Bill
  Have got no kick.
The birds that fly
  Are no more free
Of worldly cares
  Than Bill and me.

The south affords
  A winter nest;
The north provides
  Our summer rest.
Our feed, perchance,
  Comes ally carte,
But why should we
  Take that to heart?

We were not born
  To marble halls,
To silken robes
  Or full-dress balls;
But better far,
  We two were born
To dip our hands
  In Plenty's horn.

The world is long,
  The world is wide,
But we can walk
  If we can't ride;
And we have learned
  That men will give
Philosophers
  The means to live.

Philosophers—
　　You hear me, judge,
Not merely men
　　Who deal in fudge.
The genuine
　　Is he who seeks
To learn no rules
　　From ancient Greeks;

But who can sit
　　With empty hands,
Watching the rich
　　In all the lands,
And entertain
　　No envious wish—
No thought but just
　　To smoke and fish.　ˈ

What do we need?
　　Well, Bill could use
A corncob pipe
　　And two good shoes,
While you could set
　　My soul at ease
With apple pie
　　And switzer cheese.

Ah, thank you, judge;
  May you live long
And never find
  The world go wrong;
Your labors thrive,
  Your mind stay keen,
Your heart, as now,
  Be ever green.

But as for me—
  Your old friend Ike,
An idle, lean
  And restless tyke,
And as for his
  Old pardner Bill—
They never worked
  And never will.

SEX.

When woman evokes the world's applause
Men study her work to learn the cause;
She inly credits her first of laws—
   The man of her choice behind her.

In song or science, in trade or art,
The lure of her soul is peace apart,
The prize she covets a master's heart
   And his sheltering arms that bind her.

In Love's dear name, to the world's despite,
Her art is fashioned for his delight;
His smile is day and his frown is night,
   And the praise of his lips is glory.

The world has never a bay so green
As Love's own laurel that twines unseen;
But only the wise who read between
   The lines may know the story.

SAVIN' THE COUNTRY.

By jolly! we've saved the country—
　There isn't a doubt of that;
　　But the truth is, Jim,
　　I'm feelin' slim,
　For I'm lit'rally busted flat!

'Twas drinks for the boys in the mornin'
　An' drinks for the boys at night,
　　With cigars between
　　Till you never seen
　The equal of that there fight.

I fetched out plenty o' money—
　The price o' the bay an' the black—
　　But the dollars burned
　　Wherever I turned
　Till I simply can't get back.

So. Jim, as I was sayin',
　Till I get home again,
　　You could make me feel
　　Like dancin' a reel
　By lettin' me have a ten.

Ah, thank you, old man, thank you!—
  The country's saved to a charm,
    An' I reckon as how
    I'd better go now
And proceed to save the farm.

TO A CHILD.

The years stretch far before thee,
   Thy past is but a day;
Fair skies of Hope spread o'er thee,
   Love watches by the way.

As closely now I hold thee,
   Safe in a father's arms,
So may my prayers enfold thee
   Ever through life's alarms.

The tasks of Duty call thee—
   Youth has not long to dream;
In whatsoe'er befall thee
   Be thou the man thou seem.

Hypocrisy will try thee
   With promises that shine,
But keep thou Honor by thee.
   And happiness is thine.

The gauds of life may pass thee
   And lowly be thy lot;
The pen of Time may class thee
   With mortals soon forgot;

Grim Toil may long enslave thee
   Ere Nature claim her debt,
But He, thy God, who gave thee
   His work, will not forget.

NOT ALL A WEARY WAY.

This life's a weary way, my babes—
   A long and weary way;
Cares wake with morn and hover near
   Throughout the livelong day;
And oft, when thou art wrapped in sleep,
Cares still their tedious vigils keep.

Out of the all-surrounding gloom
   The grey years come and go;
Silent they pass nor ever hear
   The voice of mortal woe;
And all the store of gifts they bring
Before the happy few they fling.

These lightly sing and gaily hail
   This world all flowery fair;
For them its hours are rich with sweets,
   And Mirth the king of Care.
But O, the poor who dare not play—
They find life's road a weary way.

The many bide in want, my babes,
   Though joy seems meant for all;
In vain they call on God for aid,
   He does not heed their call.
Perhaps the Master wills that man
Himself shall frame a fairer plan.

Were toil sole price of mortal life
   It were not dearly bought;
Toil is, indeed, a solace dear
   For what we've vainly sought;
While labor holds the thoughts in thrall
Souls cease to hear their longings call.

We may not know by what a plan
   The Master holds His sway;
We only know that joys and griefs
   Alternate rule our day—
That each, His purpose to fulfill,
Must bow to the Eternal Will.

Wherefore do you rejoice, my babes,
   Ere youthful days depart;
Too soon the solemn years will cast
   A shadow in each heart.
Praise God you know it not today
How life shall prove a weary way.
  4

And yet not all a weary way;
  Some long-forgotten strain
Of springtime's music echoes back
  And makes us glad again;
Sometimes wafts back to age's hours
The fragrant breath of springtime's flowers.

THE HAPPY SKY.

At midnight in the haggard street
    Where Want and Vice together lie,
    I look toward the happy sky
While Crime creeps past on tiger feet.

Where Want and Vice together lie,
    And Sorrow hides her naked head,
    By some primeval impulse led
Hope scans the heaven with wistful eye.

O Sorrow, that with naked head
    Flees past me ghostlike in the gloom,
    Fast faring to a nameless tomb
In some great city of the dead ;—

O Want and Vice that living die ;
    O Crime by Want and Vice decreed!
    When shall man's quickened spirit read
Love's lesson in the happy sky?

Chicago, December, 1898.

SONG OF A MOTHER.

Sometimes, when dusk creeps softly down
  From out the eastern sky,
Weary of toil and sick at heart,
  I lay my labors by,

And fold my hands and close my eyes
  To sit and dimly dream,
While all life's sorrows drift away
  On reverie's silent stream.

Then I am but a little boy
  Beside my mother's knee,
Hearing again the old sweet songs
  That once she sang to me.

Happy the dreams wherein arise
  Dear visions of the past;
Ah! dear, so dear that I could pray
  They might forever last—

That I might thus through all the years
  Her boyish lover be,
Hearing again the old sweet songs
  That mother sang to me.

Some time, perhaps, when life is done,
   We two once more shall know
The pure delight that graced our days
   So very long ago;

Love's compensation shall atone
   For all the lonely years * * * *
Tonight accept, O mother mine,
   The tribute of my tears.

AT CHRISTMAS.

Christmas again!   Heigho, my lass,
How swift the silent seasons pass!

The plans we made but yestermorn
The same swift years have laughed to scorn;

The ship whereon our Hopes set sail
Hath seldom met a friendly gale;

The haven where our Longings bide
Is still upon the farther side.

But, thank the Lord!   Time's wisdom turned
Its glow upon us when we learned

That bare walls bloom beneath the touch
Of Love, that makes the little much.

Christmas again!   Our babes at play
Bring back the vanished years this day;

Yea, glad am I that Fate's decrees
Denied us gold to give us these.

And you, whose patient love hath lent
A tender grace to banishment—

The realm we missed hath naught so dear
To me as your fair presence here.

So do I bless the seasons urned,
Wherein two hearts the lesson learned

That bare walls bloom beneath the touch
Of Love, that makes the little much.

THE WAY OF THE WORLD.

Two men went down to the sea in a ship,
  Flushed with the scarlet of drink and song ;
A ribald jest was on either's lip,
  Their draughts at the bottle were deep and
    strong.

A storm arose and the vessel sank ;
  The sea rejoiced in triumphant hate,
And two fought death on a narrow plank
  That shivered and sank beneath their weight.

Then one cried out : "I must leave you, Jack ;
  You have babes and a wife but luckily I
Have none who will mourn if I come not back ;
  And one may live, but one *must* die."

"True," said the other, "my wife will wail ;
  'Tis a coward deed, but I *must* live on." * * *
Two hours later a passing sail
  Took up the one, but the other was gone.

The dull world cheers for the man who wins,
  And looks not under the sea or the sod ;
So it says of the one that "he died in his sins,"
  While the other "was saved by a loving God."

SONG FOR CHICAGO.

Chicago, Prince of Cities, I salute you
  Young leader in the kingdom of the strong:
You give me leave to labor for a living,
  I give your name to democratic song.

I owe you not a dollar—what you pay me
  Is mine by right of labor late and long:
You owe me naught, Chicago, yet I love you,
  And tender you the tribute of a song.

I do not share the whining accusation
  That art is here neglected by the throng:
True art is to its maker's soul sufficient—
  A picture or a palace or a song.

I see you honor honesty in office;
  I see you swift to grapple giant wrong;
I see you pause from trade to worship beauty:
  In each is inspiration for a song.

To conquer health and plenty for your millions
  I see your mighty Genius toiling long:
For virtue and for valor I salute you,
  Chicago, Prince of Cities, in a song.

PUTTING THE SHEET TO PRESS.

The Print grabbed hold of the lean and the fat
    And hustled them into the forms—
Locals and liners, Editor's Chat,
    And a screed on "Iowa Storms."

"Two hours late," says the Print—"no less!"
    To the Devil he shouted: "Bill!—
Go get Pete Jackson to twist the press,
    And you've got no time to kill."

The Old Man studied the proof sheets through
    And he said, with a weary smile:
"Not very fine, but I guess it'll do;
    People want facts, not style."

P. Jackson strode through the sanctum door
    With an odor of gin in his wake;
He carefully folded his coat on the floor
    And earnestly started to slake

The remains of his thirst at the battered tank
    That stood on the broken stool.
The Old Man wandered across to the bank,
    The Devil juggled a rule.

P. Jackson sighed as he gripped the wheel
   With a hold that was half caress;
"All right," said the Print, "let the old girl spiel!"
   And the Sheet went into the press.

The old press sullenly creaked within,
   But Pete was still at his toil;
"I guess," said the Print, "that we'll give her gin
   Hereafter, instead of oil."

Two hours crawled by as the hours crawl
   When the earth lies brown and dry,
And the air sinks low like a fiery pall
   And the sun hangs white in the sky.

"At last!" cried the Devil, "the last rag's run
   And wrapped and sent to the mail."
P. Jackson left with his coin hard won,
   And the boy went out with the pail.

THE RICH AND THE POOR.

The room was narrow and mean and bare
　　Where the baby gasped for breath;
The mother murmured a hopeless prayer
That died in the hell of the blazing air
For the fields of her girlhood, cool and fair,
　　While the infant fought with Death.

A wee form lay on the ragged sheet
　　That was wet with a mother's tears;
But its white soul rose through the blinding heat
That sank like a pall on the squalid street—
Ah! Death took all that her heart held sweet
　　And left her the lonely years.

O you that in purple and silks abide,
　　Had the babe no claim on you?
Had the mother's prayer at her darling's side
No power to pierce through the walls of pride?
Do you owe no debt to the Man who died?
　　Did He leave you naught to do?

Add not Fate's wrath to the human hates
    That fester in garrets dim;
I tell you the rage of the ages waits
And crouches low at your mansion gates;
Christ's brotherhood only its thirst abates—
    Go forth in the name of Him!

THE THREE GIFTS.

We thank Thee, Lord, for Thy first gift, Life;
    Precious the privilege, living to see
The race arising to peace through strife,
    Merciful, generous, chivalrous, free.

Not yet, we know, have Thy children grown
    Into the brotherhood Heaven hath planned :
But Thou wilt garner where Thou hast sown
    Plentiful harvests in every land.

We thank Thee, Lord, for life's dearest prize,
    Love that abideth while life abides;
That lightens the way to the distant skies,
    Guiding us fairly whate'er betides.

Love hath its sorrows, we know, as deep
    As its fountains of joy where we drink at will;
Yet love lives on past the dreamless sleep
    Of the dear ones out on the quiet hill.

We thank Thee, Lord, for Thy last gift, Death,
    Making for all of our ills amends;
That gently severs the fainting breath,
    Giving us over again to our friends.

The grave is low and a darksome room,
  Yet shall we enter with never a fear;
And rest at peace in its rayless gloom,
  Knowing, O Father, that Thou art near.

TROUT-AND-WHISKEY TRIP.

Going to start tomorrow—
  My trout-and-whiskey trip;
Go on away my sorrow,
  I'm going to let you slip.
    I haven't got a wish
    But just to sit and fish
    And listen to the music of the water's
      soothing swish.

Go on away with money—
  I've got a better game;
And don't you come, my honey,
  To offer me your fame;
    For I'm a-going to ride
    Along the river's side
    Until I reach the riffle where the gamy
      trout abide.

O, tell me not that duty
  Declares that I should work;
The soul is dead to beauty
  That wouldn't gladly shirk,

When river naiads fair
In unison declare
They're glad to see a fellow with his fish-
    ing tackle there.

BALLAD OF THE CENTURION.

O he has no time for to work or to play,
For he rides all night and he rides all day;
And I've heard, but I never have believed it, quite,
That he rides all day and he rides all night.

However that be, he is ever to be seen
A-pedaling along on his made-to-fit machine;
With his back humped high and his head humped low,
He rides through the mud and he rides through the
       snow.

When the old year rose and cashed in its chips,
And the new sat in with a smile on its lips,
He mounted his wheel by the light of the stars,
And reeled off a couple of century bars.

Thus ever since then he has been on the go;
He always rides fast and he never rides slow,
And he meets all remarks with a pitying sneer
And, "Notice my mark at the end of the year."

O he has no time for to work or to play,
For he rides all night and he rides all day;
And I've heard, but I never have believed it, quite,
That he rides all day and he rides all night.

MY ANCIENT FRIEND DE FOE.

Long years have sped the days I read
   Your daring deeds and bloody—
Since, safely hid behind the lid
   Of what I seemed to study,

Your thrilling tale of storm and sail
   Transfixed me with its wonders,
And brought to pass in every class
   A startling train of blunders.

What cared I then which tribes of men
   Put forth across the oceans?
On what pretext should I be vexed
   With vain grammatic notions?

No teacher's gruff and curt rebuff
   Had slightest power to phase me,
While Crusoe's skill and sturdy will
   Continued to amaze me;

Until, alas! it comes to pass
   That, just when Crusoe sighted
The foot-marked road where Friday strode,
   The teacher's cane alighted.

No lightning stroke more swiftly broke,
  Nor none more swiftly shattered;
With evil mind he stood behind
  And stoutly whaled and battered.

And then he took that precious book—
  O, grief all else transcending!
With vile intent and fiercely rent
  Its pages past all mending.

His savage glare so chilled the air,
  As spitefully he threw you
In fragments by, that straightway I
  Made sure he never knew you.

Each year that flies doth emphasize
  The loyalty I bore you;
Old Time's retreat but makes more sweet
  The pangs I suffered for you.

What else transcends the joy of friends
  Whose steadfast faith involves them
In ceaseless fear of peril near
  From which time ne'er absolves them?

'Tis even so; whiles 'neath the glow
  Of evening's lamp I've shrined thee,
Unconsciously I turn to see
  If he lurks not behind me.

Still do I dread his cat-like tread,
　His cane upraised to flay me;
But still do you, as ever new,
　With plenteous meed repay me.

Wherefore, old friend, if chance shall send
　That teacher's soul before you,
Forgive, I pray, the hasty way
　In which he one time tore you.

Consider, too the patience due,
　And let no rage run through you;
Nor be forgot his mournful lot
　In that he never knew you.

AUTO-ANALYSIS.

Lo I am but a harp through which the winds of passion sweep,
    Attuned to voice the melody of airs that whispering
      flow,
    Responsive to the ardor of the tropic tempest's glow,
Exultant with the tiger gales that down the world-
    aisles leap.

My riches are the symphonies the God of Nature
      writes—
    The lyrics sung by zephyrs in the orange and the
      pine,
    The groan of man in martyrdom beneath the sword
      divine,
The rapture of the lover on the throne of his delights.

Not mine the palace builded with the plunder of the
      mart,
    Not mine the haloed happiness of vine-embowered
      home,
    Not mine through halls of learning and of ar-
      tistry to roam,
But mine the mighty pulsing of the universal heart.

TO A FASHIONABLE POET.

Is the murmur of approval, high and higher,
  That the winds of favor waft you very sweet?

Does your spirit know its old heroic fire,
  That could laugh alike at failure or defeat?

Is the olden inspiration in your lyre
  Now that Fashion scatters roses for your feet?

Are you happy, say, or sorry, since the morning
  When, by Want and wily Patronage beset,

You began, with silken sophistries adorning
  Greed's aggressions, the repayment of your debt?

Was the offer fit for seizing or for scorning?
  Can they teach a living conscience to forget?

You are silent :—is their scorn allied to pity?
  Do they give you leave from labor now and then

To invent a gilded song or Bacchic ditty
  In the practice of a prostituted pen?

Thou eunuch of the prosperous and pretty,
  Who might have had dominion over men!

BALLAD OF THE REBEL.

I'm a link in a line from the dark to the dawn,
A little while here and a long time gone;
Shall I fight for the fallen or dog-like fawn
    On the great for a life of ease?
A plain lean rebel in a threadbare coat,
My estate is the air, the hour and a vote;
But the bread of a patron would stick in my throat,
    So I reckon I'll spare my knees.

The weapon I forge is a rough-wrought song;
It may die soon, or it may stay long
To rally the right and to harry the wrong,
    But whether it die or stay
Is of little concern to the man who sings
For he sees the finish of serfs and kings,
And he knows that deep in the heart of things
    Is the seed of a better day.

I might gain favor, as many have gained,
If I sang for the solid and frowned on the chained;
But I want no wreath that is redly stained
    With the blood of a fellow man.
For pity of the fallen whom no man cheers,
For the children coming in the unborn years
I pledge my hour to the day that nears—
    The day of a nobler plan.

TO A MOUSE IN A TRAP.

Poor trembling wretch, what sad mishap
Has brought you tight within my trap?
Had man's vile greed so clean bereft
Your bairnies that you'd stoop to theft?
Ah, who'd not lay his scruples by
That heard his babies' hungered cry?

Still, though to mercy I incline,
Must I the ends of law resign?
The crust you sought full well you knew
Belonged to me and not to you.
But—peace! I'll grant your frenzied plea,
Move back the bars and set you free.

If man one God-like spark can claim,
Then surely mercy is its name.
So, though you meant to steal my bread,
I'll spend no anger on your head,
But, warmed by gentle mercy's flame,
I'll let you go as poor's you came.

As poor's you came, yet richer far
By freedom's gift than now you are.
Your life's to me of little worth—
To you the grandest fact of earth;
So now, whilst I throw wide my door,
Begone, wee neighbor, sin no more!

A TRAVELER'S NOTES.

You are wise and your system is good—O I doubt not
You have coined the concentrate discernings of ages
Into laws that proclaim you past masters of wisdom.

I am only a stranger a little while straying
Open-eyed through your highways your customs ob-
    serving.
I shall tarry not long and I promise you freely
In the land whither presently I must be faring
I shall mention you only in praise of your greatness.

After many quick days on the way I am resting;
Here alone in the twilight I loiter, reflecting
On the miracles wrought by the cunning of man!—
On the palaces reared by the mighty, the proud,
To the glory of one whom they designate God.
He, I take it, is one of the mighty, the proud,
Since it seems he has little in common with those
Of the lowlier orders.

        Perhaps I mistake him,
But my host has assured me he rules with all power—
That the proud and the lowly alike are dependent
On his favor for even the least of life's blisses;
And I see that life's ease is reserved for the mighty.

If I err you will know it is due to scant knowledge,
To the infinite scope of the marvels awaiting,
The absurdly inadequate bounds of my vision,—
You will know and condone in your clear understand-
  ing.

I was reading this day (and it somehow perplexed me
Till I learned how the God who unerringly rules
Is allied with the tribes of the mighty, the proud)
Of a Governor's agent sent out to inquire
Into travelers' tales of the presence of hunger
In the huts of the serfs of the proud and the mighty;
How the agent, returning, reported men haggard,
Worn, wild with an infinite rage at existence,
Still dumbly respecting the gains of their masters!

And he told of one desolate, broken, in anguish,
Pouring tears—the last tribute of love to starvation—
On the pallid cold face of her perishing infant.
More he told of the pomp of the millionaire owner
Of the mine whence the diggers—his serfs—had ex-
  tracted,
Being paid as we see, wealth sufficing to give him
Lofty station as one of the favored of God.

This, I own, shook my faith in your absolute fairness
Until one of your wise men, a priest in the temple,

Quoting straight from the Word—so he said—of his
Master,

Bade me know that "the poor shall be always among
us;

Granting which, 'tis but proper they delve for the
mighty;

And 'tis well they abide in a state of abasement

Lest they grow over-bearing and question God's
statute."

"There are madmen," he told me, "who prate of 'equality;'

Sorry chaps"—here he tapped with significant ges-
ture

The abode of his brain—"vulgar knaves of no standing.

"Such as these," he went on, "would demolish tradition—

Upset utterly all the conditions established,

With their schemes for 'uplifting the down-trodden
poor.'

Arrant nonsense! my dear sir. Why, we *must* have
these classes;

They have always existed, will always exist.

It is God's holy will"—there was more, but I lost it,

For the moan of the mother appealing disturbed me.

I was thinking, too, just at that moment, of Heaven.

This seems, really, one of the handsomest features

Of the many provided for the mighty, the proud;
Such a glowing account as I heard of its beauty!
I had earlier read it was free to all comers,
To the lowly and mighty alike; but now, plainly,
I preceive this is false—clubs are not so conducted.
In these clubs you call churches—(these, you say, are
    the doorways
To the ultimate human distinction, fair Heaven)—
Here we see that the piously prosperous only
Are at home. The same law rules in Heaven, I take it.

If 'twere not an affront to my kind entertainer
In this wonderful land, I could wish that the lowly
Were provided, at least, with that measure of comfort
Bestowed by the proud on their horses and cattle;
These they do not permit to be withered with hunger.

Ah, well, it was always the habit of pilgrims,
Taking notes in strange places, to criticise freely.
But not I, for I judge that a race so sagacious,
Seeing wrong—if wrong be—will make haste to amend
    it.

BALLAD OF THE MAGAZINE.

The literary underbrush is full of splendid game,
Although the Richard Gilders fail to recognize the
      same ;
So we are going to take our guns and hunt it slick and
      clean
When Joe gets time to drop around and start his mag-
      azine.

If people here want Kipling and Dolly Hope and
      Bryce,
Why, we'll put 'em in with pleasure and we'll put 'em
      up their price ;
But all the while we're buying names, be sure we'll do
      our best
To feed the hungry poets of the big and hearty west.

We're going to get a story from the man who never
      swore,
With numerous other features that you never saw
      before ;
And articles on Purity in Politics will be
Presented by the famous Doctor Coughlin, B. H. D.

The monthlies that you buy today, from Boston or
    New York,
Are often hardly worth their weight in Armour's
    pickled pork;
Chicago's going to show you what the A1 brand
    should mean,
When Joe gets time to drop around and start his
    magazine.

MARY AND JEAN.

How oft at eve did Burns along
  The banks of Ayr appear,
A melancholy child of song,
Musing amid a mournful throng
  Of recollections dear.

The kindly after years had healed
  The wound within his breast;
Fair Jean's devoted love revealed
That happiness which death concealed
  When Mary went to rest.

He fondly scanned his bairns at play
  About the cottage door;
Toiled stoutly onward, day by day,
Obedient to honor's sway,
  That bound him evermore.

And yet, mayhap, in some lone place
  Where Ayr's clear waters roll,
His dreams at eve recalled the grace
Of sainted Highland Mary's face,
  The mistress of his soul.

6

He loved!—and who that loves today
  Shall grudge the pensive hour
When, clad in Sorrow's mantle grey,
He paused beside Ayr's quiet way
  To woo oblivion's power?

What dreams were his of pleasures deep
  That he might never know!
Perhaps, though years his secret keep,
Thinking of her who fell asleep,
  He deemed 'twas better so.

THE ARGOSIES OF JUNE.

Books lose their pleasing power
  When fairer scenes invite ;
I toast June's sweetest flower—
  The graduate in white.

Upon the toiling myriads
  I calmly turn my back,
To drink his honeyed periods—
  The graduate in black.

Each bears a cure unfailing
  For all our earthly ills ;
Each "argosy goes sailing"—
  And father pays the bills.

Their mother sits a-smiling,
  And little brother grins
As each, with words beguiling,
  The "broader life" begins ;

While I sit back a-dreaming
  Of other happy days,
When other children, beaming,
  Received the public's praise.

Wherever have they vanished—
　　To what untoward clime?
By what misfortune banished,
　　Who should have shone sublime?

I fear that Fate, unfeeling,
　　Has forced some to the wall,
Has scoffed at their appealing
　　And gloried in their fall;

That many a bold beginner
　　In life's eventful ride
Has made a hasty dinner
　　For the hideous monster Pride;

That others, gayly faring
　　With Pleasure, as they rode,
Have found him change his bearing—
　　No longer lead, but goad.

Some, mayhap, let Ambition
　　Deceive more cautious Fear,
And shriveled by attrition
　　With sterner bodies near.

Ah, well, there's no use grieving
　　Before dark days come in—
Time brings his undeceiving
　　Whether you lose or win.

So, then, away out yonder,
  Beyond the sunset land,
Let each one gladly wander
  With Fancy, hand in hand.

A REVERIE AT EVENING.

The Old Man dozed in the broad-backed chair,
　His chin at ease on his breast;
His white locks tossed in the fitful air
　That blew from the sun-lit west.

The door of the shop stood open wide;
　The paper had gone to the mail.
The Print and the Devil had stepped outside
　With a dime and an old tin pail.

I mournfully closed the subscription list
　And laid it aside for the day.
With its record of men who had "never missed"
　And of men who would never pay.

Poor men were there who in homely jeans
　Paid up for the Sheet in advance,
And men who were proud of their garnered means
　That led us a lively dance.

"Give me the man," thought I to myself,
　"Who sturdily pays as he goes;
And spare me the fellow who piles up pelf
　In the face of the men he owes.

"Far better the grip of the calloused hand
   He heartily puts in your own
Than the stilted salute, too-carefully planned,
   Of the Beat on the social throne."

And then, as the critical mood ran high,
   There came at the spirit's call
A spotted procession that passed me by,
   And I angrily judged them all:

The preacher who holily rolled his eyes
   At the greed of those sinful days,
And humbly obeyed a command from the skies
   That he leave to accept a raise;

The saint with the lean and dyspeptic shell
   Who prayed that it come to pass,
The Lord would "save from a yawning hell
   The sinner who looked on the glass."

I knew that his shaft was directed straight
   At the dear Old Man in the chair;
But he was above the malignant hate
   And the arrow broke in the air.

The Old Man's pen was a knightly blade
   That never espoused the wrong;
That never against the poor was arrayed,
   Nor truckled before the strong.

*   *   *   *   *   *   *

Those days have passed, with the boyish rage
   That tempest-like thrilled me through,
Erasing the blots on my own life's page
   Provides me enough to do.

But often I think as my pipe burns low
   Of him who was always mild—
Who governed a strong mind's fiery glow
   With the heart of a little child.

I see where the Old Man sits in his chair
   Till the sun's last rays are flown;
Peace lendeth a balm to the evening air
   And I fall asleep in my own.

SONG FOR NICOTIA.

Sweet source of a thousand remembered delights
  And of pleasing companionships many,
You have shortened my days and you've lengthened
    my nights,
  But I would not forsake you for any.

How soothing your flavor that floats in the air
  And drives away grey melancholy,
When lone in my chamber at night I compare
  The savorless fruits of my folly.

Stern friends who desert when from wisdom I stray
  I find are a valueless dower;
Fond sweethearts a-many, like blossoms of May,
  Pour perfumes of bliss but an hour.

So adieu to them all—save a lass may appear
  Who is worthy to share the devotion
I give to thee always, Nicotia dear,
  Thou spring of the gentlest emotion.

Sweet source of a thousand remembered delights,
  And of pleasing companionships many—
You have shortened my days and you've lengthened
    my nights,
  But I would not forsake you for any.

TO A BOYHOOD FRIEND.

Lamb's gossip stands neglected by ;
   The blaze leaps cheerily up the log,
While in my cozy nook I lie
   And think upon thee, dear old dog.

Dost thou recall, in that far place
   Where long time since we laid thee down,
The stately walk—the madcap race—
   Thy too-fantastic dressing gown?

And dost thou still with relish think
   Upon thy sober-comic pranks—
How thou didst smoke, with knowing blink,
   Erect upon thy shaggy shanks?

Methinks that sometimes in the spring,
   When apple-blossoms deck thy bed,
Their blooms fine memories to thee bring
   Of woodland ways we loved to tread.

And thou dost spy once more with me
   The dainty bluebells where they hide
Beneath the giant oaken tree,
   With fragrant cowslips close beside.

And haply, when the summer's heat
   Hath warmed the placid river through,
In vagrant fancy dost repeat
   The merry games I taught to you.

How well must thou recall the day
   The waters closed above my head,
And thou didst fetch me safe away,
   As one recaptured from the dead.

Thou dost remember, dost thou not,
   Our some-time playmate, little Jim?
Dear laddie!—I have not forgot—
   With thoughts of thee mine eyes grow dim.

Thou, too, art resting from thy play;
   A deep and peaceful sleep is thine.
I plod along the homeward way
   And do not murmur or repine.

But sometimes, whiles I dimly pore
   Beneath the lamp's benignant beam
Some favorite bit of bookish lore,
   I pause to nod—and doze—and dream.

My narrow cell becomes a wide
   And lovely room; two children fair
Smile up to me from either side
   As if they had been always there.

And then you come upon my view,
   As years ago you bounding came;
Thy deep-toned voice the voice I knew,
   Thy quick and eager eyes the same.

I stroke thy head that thou dost lay
   With fond assurance on my knee.   *   *   *
Before me little Jim doth play,
   A child through all eternity.

Then cometh one of angel grace;
   At her white throat a jewel gleams;
Her beauty doth illume the place—
   The saintly lady of my dreams.

*   *   *   *   *   *

Thus let me dream, nor not awake,
   So happy I in dreamland be,
Where care is lost in Lethe's lake
   And visions fair encompass me.

THE PARTNERS OF POVERTY FLAT.

There is Molly, who started with me
  On a capital shockingly small;
Helen came, we divided by three,
  And by four with the coming of Paul.

We have hopes, as what mortal has not?—
  Of delights to be finally won;
We're expecting to "better our lot"
  As so many a mortal has done.

We have youth, of all riches the best;
  We have love and are grateful for that;
Yet we're humanly hoping to test
  Something finer than Poverty Flat.

If we were not the sense of the age
  Would accuse us of lagging behind;
So I'm writing this whimsical page
  To assure you we bear it in mind.

But withal, when the day's in the bud,
  And the odor of spring's in the air,
There's a spirit of bliss in the blood
  And our world is exceedingly fair.

In the street it is restful and still
    Ere the rattle of traffic begins;
'Tis the time when the masterful will
    Is asleep and at peace with its sins.

From the view of the highway I turn
    To the sight of my babies asleep;
They have many a lesson to learn,
    They have many a duty to keep.

As I write, the miraculous sun
    Has arisen in pride from the seas;
'Tis an omen of victory won
    By the grace of eternal decrees.

It is well with today; we are glad
    For the mercies past seasons begat;
Though the morrow may prove to be sad,
    We are happy in Poverty Flat.

THE RIVALS.

The time is in March—in our temperate zone,
  When the seasons sit down—
Old Winter and Spring, rival heirs to the throne—
  And they play foɪ the crown.

Old Winter comes blustering down on the gale
  From the icy northwest;
But he's bluffing on deuces and certain to fail,
  When he's put to the test.

Young Spring saunters up from the tropical zone,
  And he merrily sings
A fantastical air in a jubilant tone—
  He holds aces on kings.

In the sheltering woods and along the south banks
  The first flowers lie low,
All ready to leap to their places in ranks
  When the lingering snow

Runs off to the creeks to go south for the summer.
  The dainty Spring beauty
Peers up through the leaves to espy the newcomer,
  And delights in her duty.

And it's little she recks of the chill wind that blows
   Through the branches above her,
For her soul is athrill with the music that flows
   From the lips of her lover.

She impatiently longs, with a burning desire,
   For her dearest of blisses—
The embrace of her love and the masterful fire
   Of his passionate kisses.

But here (as on previous occasions past number),
   Each with ardor aflame,
The players the table with riches encumber—
   And love waits on the game.

Old Winter, defeated, departs, and Spring, stirred
   By the prospect before him,
Proclaims himself king, when the flowers, at his word,
   All arise and adore him.

FAVORITE BOOKS.

When I began, a visionary boy,
   To follow Crusoe's story on the isle,
So fearful was the tenseness of my joy
   That neither love nor duty might beguile
My mesmerized attention from the page
Where man triumphed o'er naked Nature's rage.

In less delight, but having keener sense
   To note wherein the hero went amiss,
I studied with an interest intense
   The thrill-compelling ventures of the Swiss;
Made pause, betimes, to mount the hero's throne,
Recast his deeds and claim them for my own.

Came Froissart then of high romantic air,
   Whose heroes strove for honor under arms
Indifferent to weariness or care,
   Proclaiming each his lady's perfect charms;
At ease alike in castle or on plain,
So he might couple glory with his gain.

I hardly know when first I felt the spell
   Of Scotia's Prince of Singers, but it seems
   7

My memory links the Ayr with Little Nell
   Far down the misty highway of my dreams,
Commingling fleeting happiness with tears—
A heritage of fragrance for the years.

The Book of Nature, bound between the skies,
   Whereof the countless pages are the days—
I scanned its text with keen and reverent eyes
   Among the fields and in the woody ways;
Along the whispering river's winding rim
My spirit rose in Earth's eternal hymn.

'Tis but a step from love of Nature's self
   To love of Nature's loveliest—her girls;
Ah, who but, taught by some entrancing elf,
   In Love's own Book has garnered wisdom's pearls?
Unindexed joys and woes its pages throng—
Blisses that burn and pangs that linger long.

Romance and Youth departing in the night,
   The day returns to find the heart at rest;
The eager mind inquires of wrong and right,
   Delves into schemes and puts them to a test;
Ponders the words of Sages So-and-So,
On whence we came and whither we shall go.

A fruitless task: I cease and turn aside
  To mingle with my brothers in the mart,
Seeing how each to all is near allied,
  Feeling the pulse of ages in my heart.
Around me sweep, intent upon the strife,
The characters that throng the Book of Life.

ODE TO THE GRAVE.

Refuge of wounded hearts,
Shield from misfortune's darts—
  Holding us all as one,
  Blind to what we have done—
Cursing, caressing,
Sinning, or blessing.
  Mother to the motherless,
  Father to the fatherless,
    Friend to the friendless!
    Offering us endless
Peace in thy solitude
Where never sorrow's brood
  May break our rest—
  Offering us endless
    Sleep on thy breast.

Sweet shall our slumber be
Through time's infinity;
  Fairer than boreal light
  Our guardian angels bright,
    Banishing eerie
    Phantoms, and dreary.

ODE TO THE GRAVE.

Safe in thy company,
Sure of thy sympathy,
  Glad to be quit of life,
  Shut of its toil and strife,
    Naked we come:
  Only our poverty
    We can bring home.

MAKING HIS PILE.

"Early and late he is working—
    Says that's his natural style;
He wasn't cut out right for shirking,
    And they say he is making his pile."

"Married, of course," I suggested,
    "With babies to climb on his knee?"
"No; too many dollars invested—
    He's never had leisure, you see.

"No hand for sports—isn't active;
    And ask him to go to the play,
And he'll say it's mighty attractive—
    He'd be glad to—on some other day.

"And suppose you suggest that he's losing
    The joys that make living worth while.
He declares your ideas are amusing
    And asks: 'Ain't I making my pile?

" 'No wife to dispute my dominion,
    No children to go the bad;
Give me cash, in my humble opinion,
    The best friend a man ever had.'

"If you speak of the pleasure of giving,
    He puts on a cynical smile,
And remarks that 'you'll learn more by living.'
    Poor fool!—but he's making his pile!"

THE NEW BABY.

We got new baby up t' our house;
Comed last night, still's er mouse.

Found it layin' up side my mother.
Pa says 't's my 'ittle bwother.

Pa says t' w'en th' baby gets old
Es me 't won't mind any cold.

But now th' doors must be kep' closed,
Cos pore' 'ittle bwother's purt nigh fwozed.

'Taint got no close ner any hair;
Nothin' but des red anywhere.

Eyes es red, too; keeps 'm shut
So's th' light won't hurt 'm, but

Pa says 't in a day er two
He'll open 'm des like me, er you.

Pa says he rather had a girl,
Reg'ler young Wisconsin pearl;

But reckons he'll get a heap o' joy
Out that 'ittle fweckled boy.

Can't talk er nothin'; des says "goo."
Do' know 'f he means me er who.

Spose he's talkin' t' Ma; like nuff
Beggin' her fer cents 'n stuff.

Jane Ann says 't she do' know
'F she'll stay er 'f she'll go;

Says my aunts 'n 'lations all
Come a trapsin', big 'n small,

Eatin' ev'thin' out o' sight;
Keeps her cookin' day 'n night.

Ma she's des 's white 's milk—
Hand's des like a piece o' silk;

Says she's got one, two boys now.
Pa says, "Yes, 'at's so, I vow!"

Ain't got no name, pore 'ittle boy!
Er any ball, er book er toy;

'N Jane Ann says he's homely 's sin,
'T nobody else 'd tooked him in.

Pore 'ittle bwother ; 't's des a shame
'T he ain't even got no name ;

Looks so tiny 'n so forlorn,
Guess he's sorry 't he 's born.

LIFE'S "HOUR ER SO."

Jane Ann says 't baby's dead—
Says 't 'at's what Doctor said.

Doctor comed here yis't'day
'N Jane Ann says he's des gone 'way.

Nen she cwied 's 'f she had
Been doin' sumfin awful bad.

What is dead, Jane Ann, sumfin fine?
Er is 't what makes ev' one cwyin'?

I ast her des like 'at 'n she
Hugged 'n hugged 'n kisted me.

Nen she up'n runned away,
'At wasn't nice, now was it, say?

Ma she told me 't this life
'S mixted up 'ith joy 'n strife;

'T we 'd ought t' be 's good
'N char't'ble 's ev' we could,

So's 't when our time 'd come
We'd des fly stwaight t' Jesus' home.

Said when folks died they flied away,
'N all 't loved 'm had t' stay

'N wait a 'ittle hour er so,
Nen they have t' die 'n go.

How much is a hour er so?
Ma she said 't she do' know.

I asted Pa 'n he des cwied
'N said he wist 't he'd a died;

Said th' Lord 't gived us him
Had took away our 'ittle Jim.

How much is a hour or so?
I wist you'd tell me 'f you know.

JUST AN HOUR OF FUN.

What the soul o' man needs is an hour of fun,
So we fiddle and sing when our labor is done;
And we'd dance if our knees were as limber as when
We went straying with Mary and Jennie and Ben.
      O we'll fiddle and sing
      Till the old house'll ring,
And the pleasures we lack the old fiddle'll bring.

All the flowers were fair in those happy old days,
When Sage Lydia led us in botany's ways.
Ah! the games that Dan Cupid puts up on young
    men!—
It is botany now—it was love-making then.
      So we fiddle and sing—
      O we fiddle and sing;
All the dreams left behind the old fiddle'll bring.

We've a short road behind and a long one ahead;
We're but few years alive and we're many years dead,
Then let never a day be so hard or so long
But you finish it up with a jolly old song.
      Yea we fiddle and sing—
      O we fiddle and sing;
When the old fiddle laughs we're as rich as a king.

BALLAD OF THE RHYMER.

He never wrote a sonnet;
  He had no wish to try,
But sang in homely fashion
  The dreams that passed him by.

Enough for him the pleasure
  When Fancy's flowers bloomed,
No matter what the measure
  His revery assumed.

He sang of little children
  Beside their mother's knees,
Of haggard, toiling millions
  Enslaved beyond the seas;

Of all the wee, wild creatures
  That throng the flowery fields;
Of hills whence Freedom's heroes
  Came home upon their shields;

Wherever dreams might lead him
  Or human feeling call—
Along the sunny river,
  Beside the somber pall.

No intricate devices
  Of meter or of rhyme
Beguiled his pen in writing
  The common songs of time.

Rose then the learned critic,
  With countenance severe,
And thrust aloft the volume
  Upon his gory spear.

"How infinite a pity!"
  He melancholic cried,
"Of all the formal measures
  But two are found inside.

"Alas! that ever mortal
  Should wander so astray;
Thank God we live to teach him
  The literary way!"

Afar upon the prairie,
  Within an humble cot,
A weary woman sadly
  Reviewed her lonely lot.

Beyond the gray horizon
  Dwelt happiness, she thought,
And all the precious treasures
  Her hungry spirit sought.

Whileas she lingered, gazing
   Across the shoreless plain,
She sang a simple ballad
   Of love that conquers pain.

Then swift her mood was altered,
   Her spirit ceased to roam;
She saw with clearer vision
   The happiness of home.

The song she sang had never
   Received the critic's praise,
Had never stirred a scholar
   To rapturous amaze;

But there upon the prairie
   Its melody could cure
A human soul of sorrow
   And teach it to endure.

Enough there are of masters
   To glorify the art;
Give me, O God, the power
   To heal the wounded heart.

THE END OF IT ALL.

Ah! the end of it all—
    Of this life that we live;
Of the blows that we get
    And the blows that we give;
Of the joys and the griefs
    That to each of us fall—
Blind humanity dreams
    Of the end of it all.

The lover who yearns
    For affection denied;
The prince in his hall
    And the pauper outside;
The parent whose darling
    Lies under the pall—
Each mournfully dreams
    Of the end of it all.

Since God in His Love
    For His children denies
This glimpse of the end
    To humanity's eyes,

Let each bravely answer
　　Life's manifest call,
And rely on the Lord
　　For the end of it all.

THE ISLAND RACES

THE ISLAND RACES.

MURDER IN THE PHILIPPINES.

What news is this the lightnings hiss
   Beneath the western sea?
Old Glory's sons have turned their guns
   On men who would be free?

Old Glory waves above the graves
   Of that heroic band
Who proudly bared their breasts and dared
   Defend their native land?

Our fathers keep a slumber deep,
   They may not know our shame—
How Greed, arrayed as Love, betrayed
   The splendor of their fame.

But you and I, can we defy
   The judgment of the years?
Weigh well the thought time's test is not
   A greedy rabble's cheers.

My country, think that he must drink
  Who brews the bitter draught ;
When we the cup to them hold up
  Not they alone have quaffed.

My brothers, stay, ere more you slay
  To swell your masters' gain :
The land that breeds a tyrant bleeds
  Beneath that tyrant's chain.

February, 1899.

BALLAD OF CIVILIZATION.

We are out to Christianize the island races,
    (And may the Lord have mercy on their souls!)
For we'll put 'em willy nilly in the traces,
    And we'll work 'em till their sweat in rivers rolls.
        We are going to teach the savage ones among 'em
            how to pray—
          They will have to learn the motions if they can't
             be made to think;
        We have got 'em by the collar and you hear me
            when I say
          That we'll lead 'em to the water and we'll also
             make 'em drink.

You can preach until you wabble at the knees
    As to equity and like commercial drugs,
But we're bound to save the blessed Filipees
    If we have to pump the beggars full of slugs.
        Trade is waiting for the signal from the fighting
            men ahead,
          And our missionary brethren are impatient for
             the fray;
        So we're going to pluck 'em living or we're going
            to plant 'em dead,
          For we never shirk our duty when it promises
             to pay.

They have got to get in line with modern ways,
  They must sow and reap and mine and buy and sell ;
They will never see again the foolish days
When a man could face the world with easy gaze
  If he owned a cot, a garden and a well.
    For the flying car of progress has descended on
        the land,
      Uncle Sammy has alighted and has told 'em
        what to do ;
    With a bible in his pocket and a rifle in his hand
      He has started 'em for heaven and he's going
        to see 'em through.

March, 1899.

BALLAD OF THE BELLIGERENT CON-GRESSMAN.

Men of us are shooting, in an isle across the sea,
  The people who inherited the land;
Men of us are boasting, when the few survivors flee,
  A badly licked but plucky-hearted band.
    O a happy day for all of us, may we recall it long,
      When men who went to war to free a race
    Were bid, because the President was feeling good
      and strong,
      To bat our dusky brothers in the face.

"Allies of the Army" when we met a common foe;
  "Patriots who dared to make a fight."
"Ignorant and savage" when the Spaniards had to
    go—
  Martyrs turned to monkeys in a night.
    So we bade them be submissive and to trust us
      for the rest,
      In our own benign and diplomatic style;
    We would give them all the freedom that we
      thought was for the best,
      And—our guns would kill a nigger at a mile.

Having heard how Washington had fought a foreign
          yoke,
  And how he drove the English to the sea,
When in money, men and metal he was always nearly
          broke,
   "I can do it," said the foolish Filipee.
     But we mowed him down like barley with the
              vomit of our ships,
      Though the story he was game is no canard;
     For we sent him to his Maker with "My coun-
              try!" on his lips—
      It was bloody, but we had to smash him hard!

For there is no other method to convince the man who
          dreams
  That God Almighty meant him to be free;
You can proclamate and argue through a dozen dozen
          reams—
  The gun's the thing that brings him to his knee!
     So we'll hunt them in the valleys and we'll hound
              them in the hills,
      Till they crawl upon their bellies to our feet;
     It may cost five hundred millions, but the people
              pay the bills—
      And a winning war will keep me in my seat.

April, 1899.

ECHOES OF THE WAR FOR CUBAN FREE-DOM.

THE CUBAN PATRIOT.

Since slave first slew his slavish fears and dared his
    master's will defy,
The smug have damned his cause with sneers, with
    inuendo and with lie.

What time our fathers, face to face, with England's
    hired butchers fought,
They too were named a "mongrel race, to little up
    from nothing brought."

That reptile sneer is sped today at him whose breast
    for Cuba bleeds:
I call him kinsman and I say he proves his manhood
    by his deeds.

I care not whether white or black or mingled blood
    his arteries fills,
Who tireless treads the thorny track that leads to
    Freedom's sacred hills.

When time the wounds of war has healed, and grey
    oblivion hides his grave,
His greatness then shall be revealed where Love lam-
    ents her nameless brave.

MASON.

A man is risen among the cold and bloodless crew in
    senate hall;
His voice is like the voice of old, when freemen burst
    oppression's thrall.

Such words are his as Henry hurled defiant at the
    idiot king—
A speech that rang around the world: forever may its
    echoes ring!

Too long, too long, the island's green ran red be-
    neath the Spaniard's blade;
Too long the groveling and the mean the Great Re-
    public's council swayed.

Then William Ernest Mason came—electric, western,
    stalwart, free;
His utterance was a living flame that thrilled the land
    from sea to sea.

His war cry, like a lightning stroke, leapt vivid
    through the sleeping sky;
That hour a people's conscience woke—that hour saw
    Spain's dominion die!

GOMEZ.

To that high plane where Love enshrines his name
    who gave this nation life,
Unerring Time's decree assigns the hero of a newer
    strife.

His fight is that undying fight whose martyr roll is
    ages long—
The ceaseless battle waged by right against the sway
    of cruel wrong.

His arms are few, his purse is lean, the woods his tem-
    pled cities are;
His road is long, Death lurks between, but at the end
    shines Freedom's star.

Of dauntless courage, splendid skill, unwearied pur-
    pose, noble mind,
His final years are Freedom's still; youth's roseate
    dreams are left behind.

One dear desire is his alone—whose fruit pray God he
   live to see—
The hated arms of Spain o'erthrown, the land of his
   affection free!

   March, 1899.

SHOP BALLADS

SHOP BALLADS.

THE OLD FRAME SHOP

I had no time for rhyming then, nor hardly knew that
    rhymes existed ;
More useful tools than page or pen fell to my fingers
    gnarled and twisted.

While sluggish neighbors, sleeping, snored, and pious
    maid prayed God to shrive her,
Out through the old shop windows poured the music
    of my adze and driver.

With jest and song we sped the days, save some grim
    greybeard shopmate carking,
And nightly went our various ways—the old to bed,
    the lads out larking.

Who thinks of fame when hot blood swirls and rushes
    through his arteries madly ?
Who's young and meets with sparkling girls but hails
    'em blithe and greets 'em gladly ?

9

Youth comes but once to mortal man (the gentler sex,
    they say, fares better);
So frolic, youngsters, while you can; you'll soon be
    bound in age's fetter.

Then may you, chuckling, call back times when you
    cut many a caper frisky,
And weave 'em into jovial rhymes, inspired, perchance,
    by pipe and whiskey.

SATURDAY NIGHT.

Machinery hadn't as yet appeared
  And men were rated men;
No pile of metal had yet been reared
  To do the work of ten.

Before his block, from 7 to 6,
  The dusty cooper toiled,
Pausing betimes for sundry kicks
  On heading timber spoiled.

On Monday morn, with wages spent,
  And throat as dry as punk,
Each roundly swore, with firm intent,
  He'd never again get drunk.

Let others be fools, if so they chose,
  His folly was hurled afar;
"The man's an ass," said he, "who blows
  His dollars across the bar."

Nowhere, I warrant, could any one find
  A soberer set than they;
A troublesome conscience faced each mind
  With scores that none could pay.

So all week long their hammering rang
   Out through the windows old ;
And many the jovial songs they sang
   And many the tales they told.

For Toil, well fed, is as light of heart
   (And lighter, I think, of head)
As Capital, dwelling alone, apart,
   By gold's exactions led.

However that be, or false or true,
   When Saturday night came round,
The Devil had labor enough for two
   Recovering captured ground.

With cash in hand, our thirst came back—
   Old Nick looked out for that !
So Jim bought liquor for Joe and Jack,
   And Peter put up for Pat.

A burly Celt refilled the bowls
   That never were empty, quite.
Ah ! never were mortals with merrier souls
   Than ours on Saturday night.

'Twas wrong ! all wrong ! I grant you that ;
   And never again shall I
Touch glasses with Jimmy or Jack or Pat,
   As in the days gone by.

I'm happy to say such sinful ways
   Have passed beyond our ken;
Machines are doing the work these days,
   And boys the work of men.

It's proper enough the man of wealth
   Should buy his wine and drink;
The man at the block must guard his health
   In order to work and think.

Modern conditions confront him now;
   His brain must needs be clear.
The change may benefit him, though how,
   It doesn't as yet appear.

Preaching again! It's time I quit;
   Preaching's but spinning a top.
I merely intended to write a bit
   On Saturday night in the shop.

THE JOURNEYMAN.

Those days were the days when a cooper knew
   He was more than a cog in a wheel;
Then he merrily traveled the country through,
And he flaunted the rose but never the rue,
As the shops had plenty for all to do
   Wherever he made appeal.
His wage was good and his arm was strong,
   And his soul was free from care;
So he sang at his toil the whole day long,
The happiest heart in a rollicking throng,
   Finding the whole world fair.

    And on Saturday night,
    With the lasses bright,
      And the glasses clinking gay,
    The hours sped by
    Till the dawn drew nigh
      Ere he sought the homeward way—
    The dawn drew nigh
    In the eastern sky
      Ere he homeward bent his way.

He had no wife and he had no child,
  Nor ever a home for long;
And the Parson told him his course was wild—
That his age would taste like a stream defiled
If he wandered on as a fool beguiled
  By the voices of drink and song.
But his years were few and his blood was hot,
  And the lasses were fair and kind;
So he heard the Parson but heeded him not;
And I venture to say that he clean forgot
The good man's praise of the Godly lot
  And the joys of a pious mind.

    For on Saturday night,
    With the lasses bright,
      And the glasses clinking gay,
    The hours sped by
    Till the dawn drew nigh
      Ere he sought the homeward way—
    The dawn drew nigh
    In the eastern sky
      Ere he homeward bent his way.

LOVE SONGS

LOVE SONGS.

SONG.

Sweetheart of mine, I love thee only,
   Thou art the pearl of my desire;
When thou art gone, though I be lonely,
   Hope's promise fans Love's deathless fire.

When thou art near life hath completeness,
   Care's frown forgot, fear's shadow flown;
Then all life's hours are rich with sweetness,
   For thou art mine and mine alone.

What though the years their sorrows bringing,
   Some share allot to thee and me?
Always my heart, in gladness singing,
   Shall praise God's grace that gave me thee.

MARY.

Worldly gear is yours,
   Its pleasures I resign;
Heavenly joy's my share,
   With Mary's hands in mine.

Threadbare is my coat,
   Its empty pockets flout me;
Still do I rejoice
   With Mary's arms about me.

The man to men unknown
   Their notice never misses;
He finds a sweet reward
   In bonny Mary's kisses.

The great from rank and gold
   Gray Death will shortly sever;
Mary's love is mine
   Forever and forever.

IN THE OTHER DAYS.

When hearts turn back to other days
Where youth ran on in flowery ways,
Tears blot the lines of Time's long scroll
And silent sadness fills the soul.
"The other days," when time was young,
When gladness sang from every tongue—
So fair a grace the vision wears
That man forgets his present cares.
Clearly before him doth arise
A picture dear to boyish eyes;
A slender girlish figure stands
Welcoming him with open hands.
Within her eyes a light there shines
Whose meaning he but half divines;
A reverent fear forbids the plea
He longs to make on bended knee.
Fate's hour flies. They lightly part,
With sad-sweet yearning in each young heart—
A dream, perhaps, of a distant land,
Where two might wander, hand in hand.

The years that pass, to girl and boy,
Bring equal measure of pain and joy;

He out in the world at life's behest,
She sheltered still in the old home nest.
Widely apart the paths they took;
Yet she, at home in her quiet nook
Perchance, day-dreaming, may backward gaze
To boyish homage of other days;
As oft, when the world frowns cold and grim,
And the prize he seeks seems far and dim,
The present fades and before his sight
She stands as fair as she stood that night.
Then time turns back and the fragrance rare
Of her garden sweetens the heavy air;
It beareth the penetrant, rich perfume
Of her crimson rose tree's royal bloom;
The day departs, night's shades descend,
Twilight and darkness subtly blend,
And the words he breathes are a prayer of praise
For a fleeting glimpse of the other days.

A FAVOR.

O as sweet as the savor
   Of June by the river
Is the thought of a favor
   Forgot by the giver.

But the beauty above her
   Shall be forgot never,
In the heart of her lover
   Forever and ever.

SHADOWS.

O love of my heart
  In the days gone forever,
Our paths lie apart,
  We can ne'er meet again ;
Yet you shall depart
  From my memory never—
  'Tis my pleasure in pain.

Though years may prove true
  All the olden-time dreaming,
The joy that we knew
  We can nevermore know ;
I'm longing for you
  And my tears they are streaming
  Where my Love lieth low.

Long, long are the days,
  And the long nights how dreary,
Since we stood where the ways
  Led us slowly apart.
Mists that rise as I gaze
  Where you passed from me, dearie,
  Have their spring in my heart.

Could the years but return
  .That are past all recalling ;
Could the dust in thine urn
  Be restored to its throne !
But O love ! life is stern,
  And its shadows are falling
  Where I mourn you alone.

I MET A DAINTY LADY IN A WOOD.

I have been stuffed of late with classic lays,—
  Stories of nymphs and dryads, and, by jingo!
I was so won by Johnny Keats' ways
  That, though I simply loathe his Greekish lingo,
I could not quit, but read with zeal unceasing,
My new delight in every page increasing.

(I like the savage lover Nature shows us—
  The lad who wars or woos with equal zest;
No coward swain regardful of his poses,
  But one who puts his fortune to the test
Assured success will crown his undertaking,
Or new loves rise what while the old are breaking).

I met a dainty lady in a wood—
  That is to say, it seemed as if I met her,
In Keats' book—a rose in solitude;
  And sure I know I never shall forget her:
In no way like the tricksy girls around us,
Whose ultra-modest coquetries confound us.

Her glance the fires of ardent love revealing,
   Her rounded length reclined upon the sod,
Her lyric speech for love's delights appealing
   Had power to make a courtier of a clod.
Alas! alas! for these degenerate ages
When nymphs are not, save in the poets' pages.

LOVE THAT LIVES FOREVER.

Love that lives forever is a fantasy, I fear,—
Sweeter is the passion that may quickly disappear ;
Happy in the present I can yield without a tear
   The love that lives forever and a day.

Love is as elusive as an echo ere it dies,
Love is evanescent as the rainbow in the skies,
Love deceives the happy-heart, the careless and the
      wise
   With vows to live forever and a day.

Love is like the violet that ushers in the spring,
Love is like the melody the birds of summer sing,
Love is much too delicate and beauteous a thing
   To bide with us forever and a day.

FRIVOLITY.

My pen sets out to sound the praise
  Of quiet and humility;
To glorify the common phase
  Of well-behaved gentility,

When, lo! you trip before my gaze,
  Sweet morsel of frivolity,
Leading my thoughts by pleasing ways
  Along the path of jollity.

The Devil take the tiresome task
  Of teaching heathens piety!—
A savage race behind the mask
  Of civilized society.

One perfect hour I choose to stroll
  Amid your charms' variety;
A glorious hour to sink my soul
  In passion's inebriety.

Come then the smug and saintly style
  Of commonplace simplicity;
Beneath it all I'll wear a smile
  Thinking of our felicity.

I ASK NO ODDS OF MEN OR GODS.

I ask no odds of men or gods,
    But walk my way serenely;
This life's delight by day or night
    I dip and drink it keenly.

I turn my back on what I lack,
    And clasp what stands beside me;
For pocket lean and habit mean,
    Sure, love will never chide me.

But if some time she tires of rhyme,
    To prosy comfort turning,
Full well I know love's rosy glow
    In other breasts is burning.

While youth endures a new love cures
    The heart that erst is breaking;
A faint regret may linger yet,
    Long-buried dreams awaking.

But even so, need Julia know
    How ardently, aye madly,
You sought the bliss of Susan's kiss
    And parted from her sadly?

And though the pang may linger long
   Ere time the wound effaces,
By Julia led your feet may tread
   Betimes in pleasant places.

So ask no odds of men or gods,
   But seek what far surpasses—
The priceless charms within the arms
   Of Nature's lovely lasses.

PORTRAIT OF A WOMAN.

She is lithe, elastic, vital as the stallion of the plains ;
　In her bosom is the flaming of the fire that never
　　dies.
She would spur the blood to motion in a marble
　　statute's veins
　With the throbbing invitation of her long and lan-
　　guorous eyes.

When she speaks a thrill runs through me as when
　　Violino lures
　Nature's clear melodic voices from the palpitating
　　strings ;
I can hear the joyous music of June's woodland over-
　　tures,
　And the melancholy minor that the wind of autumn
　　sings.

She is Nature's child and Nature gave her likeness
　　to her child ;
　On her brow the stamp of genius is irrevocably set ;
In her heart the seasons follow—summer ardent, win-
　　ter wild,
　And her conscious power crowns her with a regal
　　coronet.

SONG FOR CECILIA.

The love that has guided my ardent pen
Has pictured thy beauty for future men ;
By the grace of the passion that thrills my heart
Thou wilt always be charming as now thou art ;
And in hearts to be a reflected glow
Shall be proof, O my own, that I loved you so—
   Shall be proof, O my own, that I loved you so.

In the years to come shall the tale be told
Of a man and a woman in times of old
Who loved with a love so deep, so vast,
That Death with reverent footsteps passed,
Forbearing to hide in oblivion's night
The rose-red blossom of their delight,
That men grown sad with the years might know
How sweet was love in the long ago—
   How sweet was love in the long ago.

SONGS OF THE CEDAR

SONGS OF THE CEDAR.

ADDRESS TO CEDAR RIVER.

Old Cedar, by your shady pools
   Where minnows hide and pickerels follow,
A truant from the stifling schools,
   As fancy free as thrush or swallow—
What happy hours have I reclined,
   A shy, day-dreaming lad, to ponder
Upon the mysteries I might find
   Within the cloud-topped woods off yonder.

The squirrel darting up his tree,
   I saw but dimly in my dreaming;
Your placid waters, rolling free,
   A mighty sea were, to my seeming;
Each gold-lipped lily near your marge,
   'Twixt wind and current lightly swaying,
Became a splendid royal barge,
   Whereon were elves and pixies playing.

What giants lurked beside your brim,
  Or met by chance in fierce contention
In that far forest, dark and grim,
  I knew them well—but dared not mention.
For men are dull and credit naught
  Not based upon material chances,
And e'en the puling babes have caught
  The tendency to sneer at fancies.

When my boy comes of proper age,
  He'll have no legend-killing teacher,
Nor any use for printed page,
  But you shall be his book and preacher.
So shall you, whispering where he plays,
  With many a pleasing secret store him,
And lead his thoughts in flowery ways
  As you do mine and did before him.

WITH MARY BY THE CEDAR'S SIDE.

Wee singers in the rural shade
  Made glad the glowing country side,
The woods their sweetest blooms displayed,
What dreamy hours I fondly strayed
  With Mary by the Cedar's side.

Sage Lydia ruled the floral jaunt
  But seldom closed her broken ranks;
Her power she had no wish to vaunt;
So I found oft a cozy haunt
  With Mary by the Cedar's banks.

Though sober comrades all designed—
  Stern bent on learning Flora's arts—
To make each flower that they might find
An added treasure of the mind,
  To me all buds were Cupid's darts.

Old Cedar, childhood's friend and guide,
  Safe confidant of boyhood's dreams,
Glad witness of the lover's pride—
Long years may sweethearts stroll beside
  Your beauteous borders, queen of streams.

MORNING ALONG THE CEDAR.

Let the laurels be worn where the fates may allot 'em;
   As I lie on the bloom-bordered banks of this stream,
Where the fish, like philosophers, loaf near the bottom,
   'Tis the choicest of luxuries merely to dream.

Here the sod is as sweet as a flower queen's crown,
   And as fragrant as hope in the heart of a child;
Here the wandering waters run murmuring down
   And my soul is by vagabond fancy beguiled.

What's the worth of the world to a man who despises
   Its contempt of the living, its praise of the dead?
Dearer far is the wood where the morning breeze rises,
   And in cool benediction strays over my head.

WHERE CEDAR ROLLS HER TIDE ALONG.

Above the wintry winds that roar
   Among the snowy house-tops tall
Visions of rural beauty soar,
   Voices of rustic minstrels call
When lo! 'tis June, the month of song,
Where Cedar rolls her tide along.

Winter is not * * *   the waters sing
   Merrily down past field and grove;
From cup to cup, on tireless wing,
   Swiftly the eager wild bees rove;
In yonder maple, clear and strong,
Red Robin trills a joyful song.

The all-defacing hand of man
   Has passed this woodland Eden by;
No blot on Nature's perfect plan
   Appears before th' enraptured eye;
Clouds wall the lovely picture round,
Guarding from man enchanted ground.
  11

Dear woods, fair fields, sweet flowers that bloom
  In many a shy, secluded spot,
Here in the distant city's gloom
  Thy gentle peace is not forget,
Nor thou who sang thy cheerful song
Where Cedar rolls her tide along.

CITY AND RIVER.

Aweary of the narrowness and bigotry of creed,
Aweary of the spectacle of cruelty and greed,
Aweary of the sorrowing of wrong-embittered need,
  My dreams are on a distant river's tide.

Aweary of the hollowness and vanity of town,
Aweary of its mighty walls that far above me frown,
Aweary heart and body of the cares that weigh me
    down,
  I turn, O mother Cedar, to your side.

Your cooling lips shall kiss away the fever in my
    breast,
Your rippling voices lull me like a little child to rest,
And all my dreams shall glow again, the noblest and
    the best,
  In waves that shine across your sandy bars.

Your beauty shall restore to me the bliss of other days,
When Joy and I were intimates in dusky forest ways,
And you and I at evening shall waft a prayer of praise
  For solitude, the silence and the stars.

"And So We Stroll to Youth's Enchanted Land"

'AND SO WE STROLL
TO YOUTH'S ENCHANTED LAND."

———

THE DANCE.

Philosophy shall fascinate no longer,
  To fathom it I've nony more desire;
A pleasure that is humaner and stronger
  Is, romping with the children by the fire.

The race of man goes on and on forever
  According to a good and proper plan;
I leave the search for reasons to the clever,—
  I'm going to be a lover while I can.

The lamp is lit, the grate is redly glowing;
  The Baby sprawls upon a pillow near;
The Daughter and the Elder Son with knowing
  And eager smiles in front of me appear.

The Mother, in an easy rocker reading,
  Upon my guests bestows a fleeting glance,
In time to note the Son and Daughter pleading:
  "Come, Daddy, we are going to have a dance."

High honor for a better man than Daddy!
   With dainty grace the lassie takes my hand;
A partner of his fancy mates the laddie,
   And so we stroll to Youth's enchanted land.

TINY TIM.

My heart is opened wide this night,
   And through its door Love's fountain streams:
   I slept, and to my troubled dreams
There came an angel shining bright.

A little child that smiled on me,
   And bade me rise and took my hand,
   And showed God's goodness on the land
And all His mercy upon the sea.

The stars that gleamed so far and cold,
   The green grain waving in yonder field,
   To my lean spirit new grace revealed—
The grave, mysterious grace of old.

For I was filled with evil lust
   Ere ever that dear child-angel came;
   And Love was but an empty name,
And Faith was but forgotten dust;

And Hope? What hope could mortal save
   With youth and youth's delusions past,
   But selfish comfort, and at last,
Unbroken slumber in the grave.

For I had fed myself alone,
　And I had pleasured on others' ill:
　Though Friendship flowered on plain and hill,
Its fragrance was to me unknown.

And time was heavy upon my head,
　And loneliness and grief were mine—
　A secret grief that makes no sign,
A loneliness of throttling dread.

And so I laid me down and so
　To me God's little lambkin came—
　Came in and thrilled to living flame
Loves turned to ashes long ago.

And he was wizened and weak and wan,
　And he was but a little child;
　But he was like a Mother mild,
And Christ-like fair to look upon.

And O the joy I got of him—
　The widening gladness that is mine,
　The love fraternal, half divine　*　*　*
God's blessing on you! Tiny Tim.

THE VILLAGE LAD AT PLAY.

What matter that his trousers bear
  A patch on either knee,
Since roses in his round cheeks glow,
While sparkling glance and light laugh show
  A spirit blithe and free?

With grimy hand he knuckles down
  To let a marble fly,
Intently scans the sphere's quick flight
And chuckles in his deep delight
  When luck approves his eye.

No mercenary gamester he,
  That craves a rival's blood;
As quick to share Dame Fortune's smiles
As e'er he is to court her wiles—
  A gentleman in bud.

He has not heard the city's far,
  Insistent voices call;
Yet not a bird in wood or field
Nests long from his keen gaze concealed,—
  He knows and loves them all.

No cares oppress or sorrows dim
  The joys his projects bring:
For all life long or for a day
I'd rather be that boy at play
  Than President or King.

POVERTY'S CHILDREN.

Some time when the Wandering Jew comes around,
We shall borrow a part of his treasure of gold;
Then we'll charter the Charity, fairest of ships,
And set off on the longest and rarest of trips.
When we've crowded the uttermost nooks in the hold
With the daintiest sweets to be anywhere found,
And the loveliest toys that the world can afford,
We shall take all of Poverty's children aboard.
Then when breezes blow fairly and breezes blow
    strong,
We shall sail down to sea with a jolly old song.
O, the babes of the poor, with the sorrowful eyes,
Where the fingers of Want have imprinted their sign—
I know what wee playthings you long for and lack;
How the little eyes see and the little hearts crave;
And I know how sad tears wet the mother's pale
    cheeks
While she stills on her bosom the little one's sighs.
Be patient, O children, be patient and brave—
God loves you—God loves you. And some time, my
    dears,
Some time, when we've waited through all the long
    years—
When we've patiently waited in hunger and cold,
He will send us the Jew with the treasures of gold.

PAUL'S CELEBRATED RACER.

The cutter stops before our door and Paul assumes the
      lines,
While Helen, from the seat behind, to nervousness in-
      clines;
She knows the cutter's wobbly and she knows the
      driver's gay,
And she has a grave suspicion that the horse will run
      away.

Their mother tucks them snugly in and kisses each
      goodbye,
Then bids the horse be careful, with a twinkle in her
      eye.
The driver shouts: "All ready!" with a flourish of his
      whip,
And off the cutter dashes at a very lively clip.

We hardly reach the boulevard (a name our street
      enjoys)
When Paul espies ahead of us a lively team of boys.
These draw the Lady Ruthie in the driver's rival's
      sleigh,
And prance along before us in a tantalizing way.

I hear my driver mutter, "Well, I like that fellow's
    face;"
"Go on!"—to me—"go lively now, we're going to
    have a race!"
With trot and pace and gallop and with sundry slip-
    pery leaps,
Paul's celebrated racer close upon his rival creeps.

"Go on!"—he shouts—"go lively Pop; we'll beat those
    plugs out yet;
We'll teach that stuck-up Lady Ruth some things she
    won't forget."
He had no sense of mercy on his puffing, panting dad;
And you bet I had to pass 'em to escape his handy gad.

But, alas for vengeful vanity, by fickle maid begot;
No sooner had we passed 'em than we struck an icy
    spot,
Whereon I slipped and scrambled till, with one tre-
    mendous jump,
Paul's celebrated racer hit the pavement with a thump.

His cutter stopped abruptly, and his rival, passing by,
Avowed that he was ready for another friendly try.
But I, rising with an effort, gave that youth to un-
    derstand
That thereafter I was out of any races he had planned.

UNDER THE BROAD ELMS.

Under the broad elms the second battle of Plevna Pass was fought. History was reversed there. Osman Pasha was vindicated—the Cossack put to rout. There the crescent waved in triumph above the cross.

West of the broad walk that divided the ground into equal parts was the favorite resort of the marble players. There Pat M. and Johnny L. waged long and doubtfully the contest that seemed never to be decided. For they were evenly matched at marbles. Never was such a daring plumper as Pat, nowhere a player the equal of Johnny in all the delicate diplomacies of the game. Neither could wholly exhaust the resources of the other, though, as we recall it, the duel, which began in the primary, ran on through the intermediate grades, the grammar school, and up into the high school.

At either of the rear corners of the square brick building stood a barrel—usually half full of rain water. Shall we ever forget that day, in the afternoon recess, when Larry D. was larruped by the principal for playfully dropping little Teddy V. into one of those barrels head first? And how Teddy scrambled out, gasping

and white-faced, but belligerent? As well expect one
to let slip out of memory the place where he learned
to swim—or where he hooked his first pickerel.

To-day the ground wears an altered appearance.
The square brick is replaced by a more imposing creation of rectangles and divers architectural usurpations.
The elms are gone. Where their broad shade invited
us to dreams or play the sun beats down upon a cin-
dered surface that grates unpleasantly under foot.

The crab apple thicket that stood half a square to the
east has been leveled to make place for a house, a dis-
mal-seeming pile, where some retired farmer, moved
to town, spends the days computing the interest on his
mortgages—a sorry substitute—with houses so numerous and crab thickets so few. Never shall that
rare perfume of a hundred trees in blossom be wafted
through the open windows on any future spring afternoon. Not hereafter shall any lad and lass, silently,
athrill with the precious fervor of young love, bear
thence the fragrant branches—spring's symbols.

The school that is now is not our school. Ours are
the older, happier scenes—the days compact of fun and
fancy—the light laughter and the hidden high aspira-
tions undertaken in Her name. Ours for to-day and
for all the years are

12

THE DREAMS OF CHILDHOOD.

His school is old, its rooms are small;
  Each ancient desk displays
On top or side some labored scrawl
  That tells of other days.

Here Jones, who quit in '63,
  Perchance when tasks were dry,
Has left a carven legacy—
  A sprawling letter "I."

The laddie learns how Jones, who "bled
  To put the rebels down,"
Came home a bearded man and wed
  The pretty Inez Brown.

There Thornton once, when lessons palled,
  And duty roved afar,
His own and Nell's initials scrawled
  Around a doubtful star.

Tradition tells how Thornton fell
  Within the battle's tide;
Of how they bore the news to Nell,
  And how she, grieving, died.

Here Wilson sat, whose young delight
  Was piracy at sea;
Alas! for mocking time's despite,—
  A pious preacher he.

So every desk its lesson keeps,
  Each mark romantic seems;
The drowsy hour that onward creeps
  Invites to idle dreams.

Eftsoon the boy is grown a man,
  His years of play are flown;
Has met what foes opposed his plan
  And left them overthrown.

The lass he, blushing redly, eyes
  With fond but furtive gaze,
Has glorified his earthly skies,—
  He wears the lover's bays.

Sail far, O child, on Fancy's lake,
  While happiness is new;
The after years can never take
  These memories from you.

The plans that gild your youthful dream
  Mayhap will never flower;
But o'er your darkest day shall stream
  The radiance of this hour.

The dreams you dream are dreams men knew
   What time the earth was young;
The song the springtime sings to you
   Has been to billions sung.

All these have sped their mortal day
   Of jollity or care,
And gone upon the distant way
   That ends—we know not where.

So do you pause, O child of mine,
   To dream a little while;
Draws near the hour you must resign
   What pleasures now beguile.

Somewhere beyond the schoolhouse walls
   Cares wait, a grievous throng;
Somewhere your manhood's mission calls,
   And you must bear it long.

But oft, as griefs oppress your mind,
   These dreams of youth will rise;
The weary world will seem more kind,
   Love's glow will light the skies.

Under the broad elms a battle was fought; it has no
place in history, and doubtless is forgotten save by a
small group of the participants, who survive, widely

scattered, yet not forgetful of the pleasant days passed
in the little village school. It has been a fancy of mine
to preserve for future generations of boys in that
school the story of

THE BATTLE OF LA PORTE.

'Twas while the Turks at Plevna Pass
   Before the Russians fell,
And while the savage Cossacks stormed
   On bastion and fort,
There came to pass the famous joust
   Whereof I mean to tell—
Now known in local annals as
   The battle of La Porte.

Four days the leaders argued for
   Positions on the ground;
They talked the question pro and con
   On playground, step and stile.
I heard it all but did not speak;
   With dignity profound,
I sat among them like a sphinx
   And smiled a deadly smile.

At last they drew up articles
   And specified a day
When Thompson's Turks should measure steel
   With Taylor's Russian band.

Thereon the generals chose their aides
  And captains for the fray,
While lumber merchants wondered why
  Were laths in such demand.

The Russian troops, full forty strong,
  Drew up beneath the elms;
They were indeed a mighty host,
  An awe-inspiring sight;
But we, the Turks, were valiant, too,
  With feathers in our helms,
And we opined that we could make
  A very pretty fight.

No ancient knights that Froissart knew
  Had armour such as ours;
No ancient armies ever bore
  So many kinds of arms.
To classify our various shifts
  Were far beyond my powers;
Each warrior felt that he, at least,
  Was safe from battle's harms.

My own equipment, I may well
  Remember it for long;
I planned it gayly, as became
  So valiant a lord.

I wrought upon it many days
  To make it light and strong,
Although be sure I felt no need
  Of armour save my sword.

A baseball mask adorned my face,
  A catcher's pad my back;
My sword-arm sleeve was padded thick
  With shavings from the mill;
My cap was full of feathers, but
  Alas! when Taylor's whack
Came down I saw a million stars,
  And seem to see them still.

"Huzza!" the Russian leader cried,
  "Now show them what you are!"
They started and we nerved ourselves
  To meet the fearful shock;
The air was rent with mingled cries
  Of "Allah!" and "The Czar!"—
Our spearmen split their fierce assault
  As water splits on rock.

The foemen, in a double line,
  Swept past on either side;
Then wheeled and, charging back again,
  Our swordsmen bore the brunt

Like heroes. "Hold your ground, my boys!"
  Our noble leader cried.
They strove like demons—all in vain;
  They could not pierce our front.

With thrust and sweep and mighty slash,
  The Russians forced the fight;
But still we gave them steel for steel,
  Still fought them hand to hand.
Our chivalry that day must break
  The Russian monarch's might
For history, for honor,
  For home and native land.

Swords clashed above the mangled corse
  Of many a hero dead;
The wounded lay like autumn leaves
  Upon the bloody plain;
Full many a hero kept the fight
  Whose every artery bled,
And often battered wrecks arose
  To shout and fight again.

Night's shades advanced with neither side
  Desiring yet to yield;
Outnumbered, smitten front and rear,
  We faced a sure defeat,

When re-enforcement, Mullan's guards,
　　Came bounding on the field,
Whereat the Russians' raging front
　　Began a slow retreat.

Each man of Mullan's giant guards
　　A massive cornstalk waved,
The roots whereof enmeshed at least
　　A quart of slimy mud;
They rushed upon a stubborn group
　　That still our fury braved
And every time a cornstalk fell
　　We heard a soggy thud.

The Russian army's slow retreat
　　Became a fearful rout;
We trailed their colors angrily
　　And flung our own on high.
Returning weary from pursuit
　　With many a joyful shout,
We marked their dead with pitying glance,
　　Our own with solemn sigh.

But O for ancient chivalry,
　　That died with ancient kings!—
How too humiliating were
　　The many bitter broils—

(So clearly all those shameful scenes
  My memory backward brings)—
When that our *slain* arose to claim
A portion of the spoils.

A FROLIC AT THE FORD.

Geography was horrible; the sweat—we called it
    that—
Bespoke a common misery when Billy signaled Pat,
Two stubby, grimy fingers uplifting on the sly;
Thereat a wink significant distorted Patrick's eye.

Then Billy turned to Cummins, and Harvey, and
    De Pew,
To each in turn displaying the grimy fingers two,
And lastly condescended, while the others winked in
    glee,
To show the mystic symbol to the least of all—to me.

O ecstasy transcending whate'er the future stored,
When Billy bade me join him for a frolic at the ford!

The hours till noon slunk by as if they knew we wished
    them past;
It seemed as though they'd never go—they did, of
    course, at last—
And O how cool the water was, and O how sweet the
    joy

That filled and thrilled the bosom of each sweaty
    little boy,
When he had hung his trousers on the nearest handy
    bough
And shut his lips and held his nose and dove to "show
    y' how."

We ducked and splashed and wrestled, we floated,
    raced and tread,
And Billy flopped his feet aloft while standing on his
    head;
De Pew had brought up bottom from the center of the
    pool,
When Harvey said he reckoned it was time to go to
    school.

"Gee whiz!" says Billy, first to quit, "that's something
    I forgot;
An' as I live! my breeches are twisted in a knot!"
Each rushed ashore and scurried to where his gar-
    ments hung,
Then sudden imprecations arose from every tongue.

While we had wooed the cooling stream, some envious
    sneak had gone
And tied our shirts and trousers so we couldn't get
    'em on.

"We're late," says Billy. "Then," says Pat, "just take
     your time to dress;
We'll fix it so's to wander in at afternoon recess;
An' each o' y' must gather a bunch o' purty flowers
An' give 'em t' the teacher er she'll keep y' after
     hours."

The teacher worked for slender pay, so far as money
     went;
She prayed and flayed and pardoned and seemed to be
     content,
And when a boy that loved her contrived to let her
     know,
She looked as if her gratitude was going to overflow.

I guess that she,—no matter what　*　*　*　when
     we six boys marched in,
Each one of us a-grinning from eyebrows down to
     chin,
And stopped in turn before her desk and laid our flow-
     ers down,
We saw two tears start sudden in the middle of her
     frown.

As I, the last and least of all, went by, with hair askew,
She stooped and said: "I love you, boys, no matter
     what you do."

"These flowers," whispered Harvey, "are not so bad a plan."

"She solid gold," said Billy; "she ought 't been a man!"

IF I COULD BE A BOY AGAIN.

I'd like to be a boy again and run away from school,
And go to Knowles' orchard, where the breeze was al-
　　ways cool,
Where flowers grew profusely, and every air was
　　sweet,
And where the striped pippins made you eat and eat
　　and eat.

With Cummins and with Harvey and McFadden and
　　De Pew,
I'd skip away at noontime, as we were used to do;
And say! we'd make the farmer boys hunt cyclone
　　caves and quake
By setting up as pirates on Quackenbush's lake.

Or, we'd play that we were miners and that Big
　　Creek's shining sands
Were monstrous heaps of virgin gold laid open to our
　　hands.
The hours they'd fly like minutes, and the minutes,—
　　well, my friend,
They'd go so fast you couldn't see where they'd begin
　　or end.

And when we'd straggle home at night, we never
would forget
To notice if our shirts were straight, and if our hair
was wet,
And if our coats had sand on, and if our shoes were
dry,
And if our backs were blistered,—you know the reason
why.

If I could be a boy again and run away from school,
I'd take my brother's old high wheel, in spite of fath-
er's rule,
And just at afternoon recess I'd make the boys feel
thin
By riding slowly past 'em, with a calm, superior grin.

Though I could make a longer jump and run as fast
as he,
And in swimming or in punching he was nowhere
near to me,
When I would ask to ride his wheel, he'd get revenge
for all
By saying he'd be glad to, but alas! I was too small.

That old high wheel, how often have I longed to sit
astride

Its slim and slippery saddle and have turned away and
      sighed,

And looked at my velocipede with dark and vengeful
      eye   *   *   *

If I could be a boy again, I'd ride that wheel or die!

JUST ONE MORE GAME.

Whoever has been a lively boy
    Is like enough to know
How very, very hard it was
    To leave the game and go,
When little brother pulled your sleeve
    And said you'd better quit,
As you had got the cow to milk
    And kindling wood to split.

Remember it? Of course you do,
    And how you there agreed
That you would take the whipping,
    If whippings be decreed ;
And how that he should certainly
    Be cleared of any blame,
If he would only stay until
    You'd play another game.

"Another game"—Ah! mighty well
    You recollect that phrase ;
How vividly it summons back
    The scenes of other days,

When Jimmy Wait and Roger Brown,
  Beside the railroad track,
Contributed their marbles
  To your capacious sack.

And how through tears that choked your voice,
  And pattered on the floor,
You later told your father dear
  You'd loiter nevermore;
And how (alas! that ever boy
  Should be so lost to shame!)
The next day found you pleading still
  For "just another game."

TO ONE NEW IN THE. WORLD.

Few words, my lad, but welcome warms them all!
    You came not like the wayside waif, unsought;
We watched the path and harkened for your call,
    And now we ask, what message have you brought?

For you what plans has Mistress Fortune laid?
    Your hands do time and circumstance prepare
To hold the plow, the pen, the ready blade?
    To smite the savage or caress the fair?

A pretty theme for speculative schemes,
    Your flower-like face within the fleecy fold;
Dark eyes that hide dim, embryonic dreams;
    A song unsung, a manuscript unrolled.

I hear men say it is a selfish act
    To call into an overcrowded race
A conscript soul by fame nor fortune backed;
    My answer is the smile upon your face.

Your trust, at least, is mine without a flaw;
    The love I give, that love you do repay;
So hand in hand, obedient to the Law,
    Let you and I proceed upon the way.

THE BABIES' TANDEM TOUR.

Fair Helen holds the handle-bars—her happy daddy's
    hands;
  The laddie, perched behind her, it would do you
    good to see.
Then off they go a-touring through many foreign
    lands
  Upon the family tandem, viz.: your humble servant's
    knee.

Through By-Low-Town and Cradle Cove they leisure-
    ly proceed;
  They view the pleasant scenery, they hear the local
    lore—
How giants thrill these quiet spots with many an awful
    deed;
  How fairies all the playthings of the sleeping babes
    explore.

From time to time a robber band appears on either
    side;
  In husky tones they hail us from a thicket or a glen.
And gracious me! you ought to see the fearful pace we
    ride;
  Not even Mr. Zimmerman could travel with us then.

The roads we know are always smooth, as roads
    should always be,
  The places that we visit we have visited before ;
But that is no objection, as you easily could see,
  If you should hear the tandem team appeal to me for
    more.

When we have wheeled past villages and cottages and
    farms,
  We stop at last beside a fence to watch some funny
    sheep ;
Then Paul's eyes close and he falls off into his mother's
    arms,
  While Helen drops the handle-bars and cuddles up
    to sleep.

"WINDY-PANTS" AND "'JELLY-FACE."

Whiles I watch my pipe-wreaths soar,
   Meditating on the day,
Comes a rat-tat at my door,
   And I hear a small voice say:
"Daddy, here's your little pards;
   Mother says we're in disgrace."
Enter then the budding bards,
   "Windy-pants" and "Jelly-face."

Paul at six is lithe of limb,
   Elfin-eyed and full of smiles;
Mother gave her grace to him,
   Gave him all her pretty wiles.
Just behind Paul, tiny Tad
   Flings his sire a sturdy frown:
Paul reflects the country glad,
   Brother, the defiant town.

Stern the Court as Court can be:
   Paul with laughter, Tad a-pout,
Climbing up on either knee,
   Tell me how it came about.

I can see that, front and rear,
   Holes in Paul's attire abound,
Very much as, yester-year,
   Holes in other breeks were found.

Brother's crime, the Court divines,
   Has to do with Mother's jam ·
On his cheeks the tell-tale signs
   Hint the wolf within the lamb.
Bit by bit the story grew,
   How the lad and laddie sinned;
Then, as silence hushed the two,
   Lo, the shameless Justice grinned!

Boys are boys, to-day as when
   Greybeards played forgotten games;
Judge and solemn Deacon then
   Went by less imposing names.
So, in my two partners small,
   Gayly I my youth retrace,
Chuckling when I hear them call:
   "Windy-pants!" and "Jelly-face!"

FRIENDS OF CHILDHOOD.

Willing sacrifice, sympathy, pleasure—all blend
With the magic of love in the gentle word friend.

The friends of old age are not many; 'tis fate
That though many come early, but few remain late.

Other ties take the place of the first in the heart,
And the friends, half unconsciously, wander apart.

Yet the few that are steadfast you feel you can trust
Until day dawns no more and the stars turn to dust.

But the friendships of childhood are rich and as pure
As the best that the future shall prove to be sure.

The birds that are nesting in yonder low tree,
They call my wee laddie away from my knee;

And, as oft as he seeks them, through all the day long,
They pledge him their love in the merriest song.

His savage cloth dog, that by day finds delight
In putting his timid pet lambkins to flight—

This terrible beast, when the shadows creep down
From the skies in the east to envelop the town,

Stands guard at his pillow, a sentinel bold,
That a mischievous fairy would fear to behold.

Right well doth he know, as he sinks into sleep,
What a vigilant watch his protector will keep;

And the rubber doll cuddles up close in his arms,
Full sure they are safe from the fearful alarms

That sometimes arouse them, all trembling with fear,
In the thought that a hideous ogre is near.

For it happens, sometimes, that the dog runs away,
And he cometh not home at the close of the day.

Then my little one prays that his Lord will forefend
What dangers he fancies may threaten his friend;

While the father bird, snug in his nest in the thorn,
Stands guard for the fickle cloth dog till the morn.

Though sorrow will come, as it comes to us all,
It is sure that, whatever disasters befall—

Whatever of loss from his life may ensue,
These friends to the end will be tender and true.

OF A DAY THAT IS DAWNING

OF A DAY THAT IS DAWNING.

There was never a mortal yearning for the life that is
    yet to be,
  There was never a supplication arose to the silent
    sky,
But the essence of God was in it,—the spirit of land
    and sea,—
  The divinely spoken assurance that nothing can ever
    die.

There was never a mortal yearning but it rose from
    the hidden springs
  In the heart of the All-Creator, the ruler of time and
    space;
And the cry of the blindest human for the bliss of the
    future rings
  Increasingly up the ages, the path of the rising race.

There was never a supplication that sprang from the
    lips of man
  But it told of the leaven working in the vessel of
    pregnant clay;

And in none of the younger epochs since the rise of
the race began
Has the passion of men so centered on the ultimate
perfect day.

I perceive that the schemes you follow are many and
ill agree;
That you pause in the joy of living to throttle and
scourge and maim,
To the end that your stubborn brothers shall see as the
Faithful see,
And shall humble themselves at the altar of the God
of an empty name.

Though the law is as music in silence or a mountain
alone in a plain,
Man has gleaned of its glorious message but an in-
finitesimal trace;
After numberless centuries pleading for impossible
personal gain,
He shall quit toil at even rejoicing in the grave's
inexpressible grace.

Not the pangs that we name dissolution, nor the shadow of infinite woe
Shall forever conceal from his vision the fact that the
race ascends

In the multiple lives of its units;—he shall see and be
    happy to go
Where the individual impulse with the source of its
    being blends.

SONG OF REVOLUTION.

Who would not give his life to see
    The race advance in kindly feeling;
The despot shorn, the slave set free,—
    God's love in mortal man revealing?
Who rates his hour o' life so high
    That Woe's appeal he hearing heeds not?
What heart when Sorrow's wailing cry
    Its armored gate beseiges bleeds not?

Old wrongs, old griefs, old days depart,—
    The old dark days of man's despairing:
New motives thrill the quickened heart,
    New love of man for man declaring.
No more the bondmen cringing crawl
    Beneath the lash like driven cattle;
The new-born freemen fight and fall
    Or win their own in righteous battle.

No more in vaunting Pride's crusade
    Can deathless glory come with dying;
The new time's hero draws his blade
    Where Freedom's holy flag is flying.

Hail! splendid dawn of nobler times;
   Hail! sun of hope in heaven ascending;
Hail! Revolution's cure for crimes,
   The chains of every tyrant rending!

EVOLUTION.

The mists of superstitious fear dissolve;
No more do I lament a fallen race.
I see that man forever tireless climbs,
A discontent divinely sprung his spur,
Dynamic aspiration in his soul,
Guiding him through the gloom toward the light.

Silent I sit within my wayside hut:
The groans of hapless millions haunt my ears,
My eyes behold the sorrows of a race:
Silent I sit, unawed by sound or sight,
Aware that this imperishable dust,
Its thousand-halted pilgrimage at end,
Shall share the bliss of Life's supreme estate.

IN THE GREEN OF OUR LEAF.

Lo, the race marches on to the measure
  Of the music that swells through the spheres;
Long gone is the Goddess of Pleasure,
With her trappings of poisonous treasure,
  To the graves of dead years.

Lust was queen at Time's morn for an hour
  In luxurious splendor supreme;
Love has brought us a worthier dower
And she leads us with tenderer power
  To a knightlier theme.

Love calls, and the listening nations
  Learn the truth from her clarion voice;
Ardent souls in all civilizations
Shall redeem us through Love's ministrations
  And all mortals rejoice.

Having youth with its promise of gladness,
  Facing age with its menace of grief,
It were folly supremer than madness
Did we dully cohabit with sadness
  In the green of our leaf.

What is life and what death and what sorrow
　　That the heart of a man should bemoan?
Have we now and still eager to borrow?
Live to-day!　Let oblivion's to-morrow
　　Have a care for its own.

What is fame that ambition, desiring
　　Its approval, should sacrifice all?
Unto Love (with nor doubting nor tiring,
As the crown of all glory) aspiring,
　　Let us march to the pall.

Love for all of humanity's creatures,
　　Yea, a love that is proof against fears;
So our thoughts that survive shall be teachers
And our deeds be the text of Love's preachers
　　Through the infinite years.

A CRY IN THE DARKNESS.

Against the bars of blindness beating,
   Entrapped for time's eternal day,
By neither life nor death completing
   Toil's ceaseless round, we keep the way.

O life, O love, O deathless yearning!
   Mid fearful gloom we walk alone.
From dust up-sprung, to dust returning,—
   Thou God! when shall Thy will be known?

THE PURPOSE OF LIFE.

Do the tears that arise in the heat of the strife
Seem to hide from your vision the purpose of life?
Do the myriad cares of laborious days
Leave the doubt in your heart whether living them
    pays?

Banish doubt and plod on: Life was given to man
As a part of Creation's mysterious plan;
Each must carry what burdens the years may bestow
Until burdens and bearer alike are laid low.

At the end of the road is a couch with a pall,
And it may be the couch is the end of it all;
Or it may be the spirit, released from the clod,
Shares the freedom of Time with the infinite God.

'Tis but folly to dig into moss-covered creeds;
Let your life be a record of generous deeds.
Not the wisest may fathom Futurity's plan,
But the weakest may live as becometh a man.

SACRIFICE.

He who for an immortal life adopts a mortal creed
Proclaims alone the littleness of egotistic greed.

Enough it is, as sure it is, that ere I reach my goal,
Some deed of mine shall glorify the universal soul.

Light! give us light that we may know the grandeur of
    the plan
Wherein all seen and unseen growths are common heir
    with man.

This blade of grass whereon of late some careless
    passer trod,
Is flesh of mine and soul of mine and part with me of
    God.

The witless scoff, the willful blind fling maledictions
    wide,
But Truth triumphant keeps the way with unimpeded
    stride.

Time proves all things, defines all things, assorts, ac-
    cepts, rejects;
The years a single sermon preach, with sacrifice the
    text.

O man, O woman, heed ye not the anguish of the rod,
But learn the bliss of sacrifice, that proves the man a
     god.

AN ARMY ON THE WAY.

The race is but an army on the way
From primal Night to truth's eternal Day.
   The journey done, we'll dwell together long
As brothers under Love's benignant sway.

In every corps one holds supreme command,
Commissioned from the all-Creator's hand,
   Assumes the air and station of a god,
And leaves a gospel regnant in the land.

Each mighty leader all the rest denies,
Yet each proclaims the Spirit of the Skies,
   Rewards with hope the multitude behind
And frowns upon the prematurely wise.

To each in turn the God enough reveals
To serve a little time, the rest conceals,
   In tender mercy answers not at all
Presumptuous man's perpetual appeals.

Deluded aye, each solemn zealot peers
Adown the crowded pathway of the years,
   And prophesies for pleasure taken now
A limitless futurity of tears.

The God of All is good; he doth decree
Immortal life divine for you and me;
    The law is writ in living letters large
Alike upon the continent and sea.

I love you all, Mohammedan or Jew,—
Whoever says his creed alone is true,—
    For we are way-worn comrades and I go
To share a splendid destiny with you.

IN THE DAY OF DEMOCRACY.

Have you hate in your heart for a mortal, my brother?
  Do you envy the victors the crowns they have won?
Time will show you all mortals made one with each
    other
  In the day when the will of Democracy's done.

In the day when the will of Democracy's done,
  You and I, in the dust of dead centuries sleeping,
Will be there in the person of daughter or son,
  All the fruits of our earlier sacrifice reaping.

All the fruits of our earlier sacrifice reaping,—
  In the ultimate hour possessed of our own;
For the God of creation has man in His keeping,
  And be sure we shall reap from the seeds we have
    sown.

THROUGH THE SPIRIT'S CALM EYES.

Men are sick with unsatisfied yearning,
   They are chilled by the shadow of fear;
They would learn what is past human learning
Ere the dusk of their day shall appear,
So with prayers that are ever returning
   Unappeased from vacuity's ear,
Or with logic high heaven assailing
In a quest that is vain, unavailing,
   They are borne to the bier.

Earth but serves for humanity's training,
   'Tis the path of the race, not its goal;
Through the years nobler attributes gaining,
   Individuals leaven the whole;
Love eternal, her kingdom attaining,
   Shall perfect us from pole unto pole.
Though earth die when its mission be ended,
Yet the spirit of man shall be blended
   With the Infinite Soul.

At the end of all lusts, of all laughter,
   At the end of all moans and all sighs

Of our sons and all men who come after,—
   When the earth wanders cold in the skies,
Or, bereft of what destinies waft her,
   On the floor of the universe lies,—
We shall see, being healed of our blindness,
The mysterious ways of God's kindness
   Through the spirit's calm eyes.

CREED.

My doubts depart, my hopes are flown—
   When hope is not fear's horror flies;
This life is mine—this life alone;
   The creed that claims another lies.

To-day, to-morrow, days to be,
   The eternal Now together make;
The laws that framed the thou and me
   Shall back to Nature's bosom take.

By whatsoever of good or grace
   The thou and I bestow on man,
In so much more the ascending race
   Approximates the perfect plan.

I have no feud with man or God,
   I care not what the creed you claim;
That path the buried billions trod,
   Your feet and mine must tread the same.

The way is clear, the law is plain,
   A myth deceives the pagan hives;
Seek thou this hour the race's gain,—
   The race and not the man survives.

I face the darkness unafraid,
   Great Nature's peace my bosom's guest;
By labors done my debt repaid,
   By sorrows taught the bliss of rest.

"WHERE ALL SORTS SIT AT THE BOARD TOGETHER."

18

"WHERE ALL SORTS SIT AT THE BOARD TOGETHER."

BALLAD OF WATTS' BILLY GOAT.

You talk about your two-wheeled bikes
　　With patent rubber tires,
With shiny spokes and padded seats,
　　That all the world admires;

But I remember well a time
　　When three wheels met my need,
And say! I caught the public with
　　My old velocipede.

When Skinny Watts' billy goat—
　　His master's joy and pride—
Came drawing Skinny down the street,
　　I'd wheel up to his side;

And I would say, says I, "My boy,
　　Your goat is getting old."
Says Skinny, "He can beat your rig
　　For marbles, chalk or gold."

Gee whillikens! the fun we had!
 And how that goat did race,
While Skinny's coat tails flapped the wind
 Before my eager face.

With fast and ever faster tread
 I pushed the pedals 'round;
My breath it came and went so hard
 I heard no other sound.

With many an anxious glance ahead
 Along the rutty track,
My rival's reinsman plied his whip
 Upon his racer's back.

First I would gain, and then the goat—
 Inspired by Skinny's whacks—
Would shake me off as if I had
 Been anchored in my tracks.

As we approached the finish line,
 Where, packed in triple ranks
The people stood, my wheels were close
 Beside the billy's flanks.

Determined now to do or die,
   I summoned all my strength,
And though the billy did his best,
   I led him home a length.

*   *   *   *   *

The goat has gone unto his rest—
   I mind the day he died—
And how we youngsters buried him,
   And how we softly cried;

And how poor Skinny's heart was sore
   For many and many a day,
For thinking of his trusty pet
   That death had led away.

But time, that gives, doth also heal
   The wounds he wanton makes,
And Skinny—beg your pardon, Judge—
   Now drives in stylish brakes;

While I, as in those happy days,
   The silent steed best like;
Wherefore my old velocipede
   Was followed by a bike.

WHERE NATURE WAITS.

Let social rank and pride of place
   Be held by them that seek and prize 'em ;
So I find smiles on nature's face,
   These paltry baubles, I despise 'em.

The idle fair of folly's code,
   I have no wish to disabuse 'em,
Nor set upon a manlier road
   The fops whose trade is to amuse 'em.

The humblest flower amid the grass
   Is worthier thought, in my opinion,
Than any laced and perfumed ass
   In pompous fashion's dull dominion.

Let honest toilers bless their lot,
   Nor let the painted show deceive 'em,
For worth is not where toil is not—
   And idle hands have ills to grieve 'em.

Where lovely nature's open arms
   Await but your desire to bind you,
Go walk 'midst her abounding charms
   And leave all envious hates behind you.

THE INDIVIDUAL.

Look neither down nor up, my friend, to vice or virtue
　　find;
For signs of growth look neither before you nor
　　behind:
Lo, every earthly mortal unconsciously within
Gives room to every virtue and room to every sin.

WALT WHITMAN.

(To J. G., with a copy of "Leaves of Grass.")

A democrat of democrats—a man!—
  A mighty seer amid the sons of song;
He grasped entire the scope of Nature's plan,
  Seeing that all is good and nothing wrong.

He glorified the spirit of the west,
  Withheld no meed of merit from the past;
He saw with prophet vision that the best
  Of time's reluctant blessings is the last.

Too great to heed the trammels of the schools,
  Wherein the plodding scribbler serves his day;
Indifferent to the mockery of fools,
  He led the race in Love's appointed way.

UTAH.

I.

Strange people, these Mormons that were.
Caught up in the net of Smith's creed,
The starvelings of Europe's big towns
Came over by ship loads, like sheep;
Recruits left lean farms where the soil
But barely supported men's lives.
A few came with money, and some
Who had culture exceeding their wit;
Yet others foresaw in the church
The means of advancing their fame.
These were led—these and others—by men
Who saw with fanatic prevision
An empire built in the west—
Themselves as its masters supreme.

II.

They journeyed past rivers and plains;
They climbed the dark mountains and filed
Through the passes the Indians knew.
God had frowned on the land where they stopped;
It parched under harrowing suns.
The sage brush and grease wood were there,

And the cactus snarled up from the sand,
But men could not live there—till then.
These Mormons, however, were stern;
They watered the plains with the snows
That melted and ran from the ranges,
They plowed, and they planted—and prayed;
And they reaped, for the soil teemed with gold
That needed but water to fuse.

III.

More came across seas, and their priests
Made converts throughout all our east.
Polygamy peopled the plain, and its masters
Grew proud.   And pride ever was blind.
They builded on ignorant hope,
On vain superstition and fraud,
On hunger, on fear and on lust.
They thought that the church could so weld
Its people together in time
That the ceaseless wave-beating without
Of a civilization more pure
Could never disintegrate them.

IV.

Monogamists saw that the land
The Mormons had settled was good.
They entered thereon and they dropped

In the ripening soil of the minds
Of the children of Mormons the seed
Of a higher spiritual life.
What's the fruit of it all?   Well, to-day
This land that the Mormons reclaimed
Comes into the Union—a State—
A sister to Maine and Montana,
To Delaware, Texas, Ohio—
Well worthy the welcome they give.
Polygamy skulks in the rear,
Disowned by the best of its sons—
Disowned by the church that it built!

V.

Time's alchemy baffles the wisest:
Here's good sprung from evil direct.
What good?   Well, a desert made green;
A tribe of good men come to life
From the loins of polygamous sires;
A new star in the flag; a new step
To the ultimate union in one
Of all hopes of this nation of ours.
   1895.

THE BAD LITTLE BOY.

The busy little neighbor boy
  Improves each shining hour
By doing all the naughtiness
  That lies within his power.

He "plays for keeps" and daily wins
  Our darling's toys away;
And, O the sinful words that he
  Has taught our child to say! ‹

All this, perhaps, I might endure,
  But I *must* draw the line
When that *his* mother says *her* son
  Learns wickedness from mine.

THE SINGER SLEEPS.

(Lines written on the death of Eugene Field.)

The magic pen is rusting, and the page
Awaits a touch that it shall never know.
The gentle hands are folded on his breast;
The shadowed chamber somber silence keeps;
Tread soft without, speak low—the singer sleeps.
Fair fall what dreams illuminate his rest,
The chosen friend of childhood and the sage,
Through all the tireless years that come and go;
And in God's time be his the tender joy
To be awakened by a Little Boy.

THE SPIRIT OF CHANGE.

I.

The calm stars looking on men see all
  Aspire to power or wealth or fame;
And each one comes at the Spirit's call,
  Through paths of peace or by roads of flame.

II.

The great town's treadmill servants dream—
  So dear God lightens their want and gloom—
Of joys that beckon by sunlit stream,
  In whispering fields and orchard bloom.

III.

The young man hears, in forest or farm,
  The Spirit's challenge and hotly frowns;
Then wood and meadow have lost their charm—
  He pits his powers against the town's.

IV.

To men grown weary of age-old wrongs,
  In king-ridden lands past far-down seas,
The Spirit speaks in fiery songs
  That smite and shatter unjust decrees.

V.

West, west and always westward pour
  The lean hordes sired in alien hives—
An endless surge through Freedom's door:
  They sow the desert and lo, it thrives!

VI.

A strong race heaping their riches high,
  Lords of a continent, land and tide,
Leap into regiments, hearing the cry
  Of Progress fighting on earth's far side.

VII.

So hatreds perish; so peoples merge;
  So Truth has ever a newer birth;
While strong men moved by the Spirit's urge
  Spread Love's Republic over the earth.

A SUMMER DAY.

Whilere the sun hath risen from the sea
The cock's alarum wakes the sleeping farm,
The good wife riseth and the sluggish boys
Turn, grumbling mildly, from their downy couch.
Beyond the lane, snug under willows housed,
The heavy cattle stand and 'gin to graze;
The horses whinny shrilly in their stalls;
Mine old friend Tray stalks stiffly from his hut;
The eager swine proclaim the coming day
By calling loudly for their meed of corn.
The monarch sun, ere that he comes to view,
Hath paled and purpled all the eastern arch;
He drives the stars, 'night's sentinels, from the sky
And last their queen, fair Luna, doth depose.
Again, what while I drive toward the field,
Ariseth to the cloudless dome of blue
The ancient rooster's "cock-a-doodle-doo!"

My wagon rumbles past the osage hedge,
And past the pond whose banks blue lilies fringe;
I note the drops of dew, which, like fair gems,
Do sparkle on their petals; and I see
Where, near the farther shore, a wild duck feeds,

A rising gentle breeze doth stir the flags
And toss with airy grace the corn's green plumes;
The sun's bright rays do heat the placid air
Until the world seems wrapped in waves of light;
Whiles to and fro my horses draw the plow,
Betimes a rabbit darts across my path;
Or Master Squirrel cocks his pretty head
And gazeth slyly on me ere he turns,
Evanishing as stilly as he came.
The sun sails upward to the middle day;
I crave a cooling flagon from the well,
When calls across the fields the welcome bell.

When wife and I and our two sturdy sons
Are seated at the plain but bounteous board,
I ask God's grace upon our food, our toil—
Beseeching Him that He will give us peace
What while we live, and in the end will close
Our days in hope to bide with him for aye.
The noon time passes quickly and I go
Back 'midst the corn and labor till the eve.
When that the shadows slant athwart the earth,
And Sol doth sink into the western sea,
I leave the plow and turn my team toward home.
The evening meal dispatched, our boys depart
To call upon the neighbor youths hard by;
The stars return to watch throughout the night,

And she, their queen, resumes her vaulted throne;
Thus, while she floods in radiance all the land,
My wife and I sit silent, hand in hand.

FISHING SONG.

Come, boys, get down your dusty poles,
  Your reels and flies and lines;
We're off to where the Brule rolls
  Among the northern pines—
To where the sparkling Brule rolls
  Among the fragrant pines.

The ice is gone; the river flows
  Serenely on her way.
(But whether south her current goes
  Or north, I cannot say;
I only know the whisky flows
  The old familiar way.)

Before our tent beside the stream
  We'll sit and smoke at eve;
The nights shall pass with ne'er a dream,
  The days with naught to grieve—
Clear nights whereon the pale moon's beam
  Shall linger loath to leave.

The fish?   Alas! again must I
    Confess I know them not.
Guides named them all when I was by
    But I have clean forgot;
(Or else the poteen held my eye
    So that I heard them not.)

Enough it is that I declare
    Earth has no fairer scene—
No joy not held in that crisp air
    Deep in the wildwood green,
Where gleams the Brule debonair
    Her vineclad banks between.

So come get down your fishing poles,
    Your patent reels and lines,
And we'll go where the Brule rolls
    Among the northern pines—
To where the sparkling Brule rolls
    Among the fragrant pines.

SINNING AND REPENTING.

The dull routine of daily life,
   It palls upon the best of us;
They find the narrow path too tame—
   And jump it like the rest of us.

Old Adam's taint that stirs the blood
   Demands a roaring hour of us;
We know it's wrong, but to deny
   Its plea's beyond the power of us.

So off we flit, with happy hearts
   To where inspiring spirits be;
We laugh and sing and swap old yarns
   With e'er increasing gayety.

Braw Bobby weaves a fearsome tale
   Of mysteries all new to us,
While Tommy's artful tongue unfolds
   Full many a pleasing view to us.

'Twixt pipe and bowl our joy ascends,
   But sad, O sad's the fall of us,
When, wandering home at break of day,
   Reproaches welcome all of us.

With tears and with a lecture keen
   The good wife stirs the soul in us,
Till we resolve henceforth to tread
   No path but that of holiness.

NIGHT AND DAY.

Whenas my clay
Slumbereth from the day,
My soul goes out where ransomed spirits play.

The clock within the tower
Tolls midnight's hour,
As swift I fly past forest, field and flower.

Joy!—joy to flee
From that which burthens me—
From all its ills and crosses to be free.

The weary day
Too long, too long doth stay,
But like love's hour the night doth speed away.

PROGRESS.

Since Epictetus spread the rays
   Of Reason's lamp around,
The human race, by stony ways,
   Has moved to higher ground.

That time the lauded attribute
   Was courage to endure;
To-day's evangels substitute
   An inquiry and cure.

When Arrianus' pencil caught
   The master sage's speech,
He felt that biting, pungent thought
   All time the truth would teach.

Here—here, he said, was logic's end—
   Life's ultimate decree;
Statutes the years could not amend
   Through all eternity.

So deemed each one whose brain defined
    A nobler moral code;
But, lo! the years left all behind,
    Debris beside the road.

Left all behind?   Well, hardly all;
    Rather from each they took
What living brands old creeds let fall
    And all the dead forsook.

And so to-day the ardent souls
    That preach the latest creed
Are very sure their scheme controls
    The race's final need.

Enthusiastic, unafraid,
    Combative men are these,
Spreading the word, in faith arrayed,
    Beyond the farthest seas.

I would not by or speech or pen
    Their glorious zeal abate
Whose lives of love proclaim to men
    The mockery of hate.

And yet—and yet—time's teachings show
   Some day beneath the sun
A fairer plan than aught we know
   Will prove Christ's labor done.

Not soon—the long, long years will fade
   Ere Time shall bear the hour
When every human heart is made
   To feel the Martyr's power.

But in some period, distant, dim,
   The eyes of man shall read
The perfect purpose writ by Him
   Who scattered here the seed.

NIGHT ON THE PRAIRIE.

Alone on the limitless prairie—
On a borderless sea of prairie.

Yet not all alone, for the stars are above
    And pale daisies float on the ocean of green;
Not alone, for the Spirit of Infinite Love
    Fills and surrounds the whole magical scene;
Fills and surrounds it with wonders unending,
    Tempers and softens the crystalline light
Of the moon, that, in luminous splendor ascending,
    Gazes like a goddess on the night.

Night and the silence of death on the prairie—
On the star-studded stretch of the prairie.

Silence that weighs like a stone on the soul;
    Of a tomb whence the spirit has arisen in the night;
Or a frame whence the ego has gone to its goal;
    Or the grave, when, life's vanities faded from sight,
Soothed into stillness by Lethe's embraces—
    Forgot all our past, all its dark misbehavior—
We sleep in the dust of unnumbered dead races,
    Awaiting the loving command of our Saviour.

Here, far from men, am I near to my Father—
Thrilled and inspired by His manifest presence.

Out of far space, down through æons of ages,
  Steals a divinely melodious strain—
Nature's grand harmony. Peasants and sages
  Hear it in solitude oft and again.
All earth life feels and is glorified by it,
  Beauty has in it an alpha divine;
Gladness springs up in the heart melted by it—
  Gladness in beauty how doubly divine!

NIGHT IN THE WOOD.

I'm alone in the wood, with its legend and story,
  In the trees is the murmur of wind and of rain;
And I'm thinking how hollow a bauble is glory,
  How poor the ambition that's fixed upon gain.

Hush! a bird-note in plaintive remonstrance ascend-
      ing;
  Over yonder the waters rise up to the mist,
And the gray of the eve with night's blackness is
      blending,
  When—again that sweet even-song—list to it!—list!

O my soul, may the voice of the Father come calling
  To His children at eve with as tender a tone;
And as now may the tremulous shadows in falling,
  O'er our faults in like generous mercy be thrown.

www.ingramcontent.com/pod-product-compliance
Lightning Source LLC
Chambersburg PA
CBHW021958050726
47498CB00006BA/1818